A RED ... FRONT OF MY EYES....

Flashes—images—mental pictures tried to come into focus. Somebody was in my apartment. I groped on the desk for my large black flashlight. Then I slipped the Walther PPK out of its holster.

Danger. Rolling misty red.

I took three steps into the deep shadows of the apartment and that was when my foot nudged against Denise's ankle. I clicked on the flashlight and played the beam over her face and body. They'd tortured her. Her beautiful, aristocratic nose had been broken and her eyes had been viciously blackened. From the bruises on her neck, I assumed she'd been strangled.

And then I saw him. Not a strong mental image but enough to identify him. Somewhere in the apartment. Right now.

The bedroom. It was the only place he could be. I went through the door as if I had no suspicion he was hiding behind it. When I was four or five steps into the room, he lunged at me. I turned and swung the butt of my pistol and felt a satisfying crunch. He leaned a little bit forward, just as I was starting to swing again, and sprayed me directly in the face with some kind of chill crystal mist. And suddenly all of my senses began shutting down at once.

I heard myself hit the floor, and then I heard nothing at all. . . .

THE FUGITIVE STARS

DANIEL RANSOM

DAW BOOKS, INC.
DONALD A. WOLLHEIM, FOUNDER
375 Hudson Street, New York, NY 10014

ELIZABETH R. WOLLHEIM
SHEILA E. GILBERT
PUBLISHERS

First Printing, July 1995
1 2 3 4 5 6 7 8 9

DAW TRADEMARK REGISTERED
U.S. PAT. OFF. AND FOREIGN COUNTRIES
—MARCA REGISTRADA
HECHO EN U.S.A
PRINTED IN THE U.S.A.

This one is for Lynn Lawrence
for being such a great brother-in-law

ACKNOWLEDGMENTS

This book could not have been written without the extensive help of Larry Segriff.

This novel owes various debts to the Saturday matinee magicians of my Midwestern boyhood:
Don Siegel
Jack Arnold
Val Lewton

ONE

ONE

EYES ONLY
HAND DELIVER: TO DAVID FITZHUGH
FROM: COL THOMAS RODHAM
RE: Spirochete

David—
   I am sending along the records that
prompted my little one-man investigation into
this *Borrelia burgorferi* business, which I al-
luded to on the phone yesterday morning.
   I think you'll see right away what I mean
about the personnel involved. If anybody ever
finds out that I copied these records and
gave them to you, my tit's in a wringer and
so's yours. The folks upstairs were exceed-
ingly pissed when I questioned them about it.
I need some real scientific help with this, David. I hope you'll help.

   T.R.

And so it was on a snowy Thursday afternoon—
with five inches of the white stuff predicted—

that a balding forty-three-year-old biochemist
named David Fitzhugh started looking through
the records his Pentagon pal Colonel Rodham
had sent along.

Fitzhugh was in a biochemical laboratory out
near the Naval Oceanographic Office in the
Washington, D.C., area.

Fitzhugh's latest work involved the mechanism of several different enzyme molecules and
the role they played in speeding up chemical
reactions.

Rodham's work sounded like a lot more fun.

Inside the folder, Fitzhugh found photographs of six people, plus two pages of medical
commentary on each. The medical commentary
ran largely to a behavioral study of each individ-
ual.

There was an attached sheet, written by Rodham, about a spirochete called *Borrelia burgorferi*
and the odd resemblance it bore to the curious
rash each of the six people showed on the inside
of his or her right arm. Rodham, who was a medical doctor, said that while this particular *ery-
thema migrans* superficially looked like Lyme
disease, it was not Lyme disease. He wanted to
know what it was. Exactly.

Fitzhugh set to work, wanting first to learn
something about the biopsy sample Rodham
had included with the folder.

Two hours later, Fitzhugh used a radioactive

isotope to study the chemical reactions in this particular organism.

He was excited and deeply confused.

More hours elapsed. He didn't hear any of the heavy yellow monsters trying to scrape the streets clean outside; nor did he watch the theatrics of the TV weatherman as he declared a snow emergency nor witness any of the dozens of fender benders taking place on the various freeways.

He was too busy; and having too much fun.

What the hell did he have hold of here, anyway?

He took a break, heating up a cup of coffee in the small microwave and pulling down some of his loftier textbooks. He was going to need a whole hell of a lot of lofty textbooks by the time he found his answer.

It was at this point, 10:02 PM, EST, as Fitzhugh sat with his feet up on the desk and a pencil sticking out of his ear (out—not behind), that a gloved hand tripped the lock on the exterior door of Fitzhugh's lab, and a man dressed completely in black, right down to the silencer on his Ruger and the ski mask over his head, eased open the inside door and took a long hard look at the man with his feet up.

"He didn't do you any favors, Mr. Fitzhugh."

So engrossed had Fitzhugh been that not until that moment did he realize that he had a visitor.

His feet came down from the desk. He stood up, making a show of making fists. But actually his bowels were cold and sickly things, and his heart was pounding with humiliating fervor.

"He shouldn't have shown you those files," said the man in the ski mask.

He shot Fitzhugh twice in the face, twice in the chest. Then he went about making it look as if a robbery had taken place, drawers yanked out and overturned, the floor and desktop a blizzard of scattered papers.

Not Colonel Rodham's files, of course. Oh, no. Those were tucked safely beneath the right arm of the man in the ski mask, along with the tissue sample.

Who looked around one last time.

Who seemed quite pleased with his work.

Who glanced down at Fitzhugh and then put another bullet in the biochemist's temple. Why take chances?

Then he was gone, into the wailing blizzard that was about to shut Washington, D.C., down for a good twelve hours.

1

December 3, 2011

They said the first mission was jinxed. This was the second mission, and if anyone had asked Captain Wendy Abronowitz, she'd have said this one was jinxed, too.

They were eight weeks out, more than half-way through the return leg of their trip. Another twenty-one days would see them touch down once more on the green, green hills of Earth. That is, if they made it that far.

The first part of their mission had gone smoothly. Their mixed crew of six astronauts—two Americans, two Russians, a French bio-physicist, and an Israeli—had been sent out to examine a comet as it once more flew by the Earth on its way out of the system. Just as the earlier mission had been sent to observe it on its way in.

That first mission, led by Captain Jack

Campbell, had also gone smoothly, right up until they reached the comet. After that, things had gone sour. Not many people knew exactly what had happened, but the rumors were terrifying.

And now Wendy, having watched her own team investigate the comet, and having seen what happened to them, knew that the rumors were nowhere near terrifying enough.

2

December 3, 2011

At the same time on Earth, the early edition of *The Washington Post* was just appearing, carrying a small but front page story about one Colonel Thomas Rodham, who had been missing for six days and whose wife feared he had been depressed about being passed over for a Pentagon promotion.

Rodham had been found in a Langley, Virginia, motel. Alone. A bullet having ripped through his mouth and exploded the back of his head. Suicide, of course.

Services were pending.

3

Captain Jack "Cap'n Jack" Campbell was a good team leader. He'd headed up several near-Earth missions for NASA, and led one of the early joint NASA-EEC moon missions a decade earlier. He had an amiable style of leadership, but everyone under him knew he could be tough when the situation demanded it.

Officially, he was supposed to be retired from active duty, but he'd called in a few favors on this one. Imagine, a comet that defied all known behavior patterns of comets; one that had no corona and no tail and so was completely invisible from Earth, even from less than a million miles away. This comet, cataloged as C2007G, had only been detected by accident. One of the filters on the Hubble II had failed to kick in, and the resultant image showed C2007G streaking across the picture.

There'd been a lot of arguments in all the usual circles: Was this really a comet or merely an asteroid with an unusually large orbit? That was one of the questions this mission was designed to answer. The fact that the orbit took the traveler out beyond the Oort cloud was enough for most people to call it a comet.

And Jack had a thing for comets. Like most kids, he'd had a passion for dinosaurs when he was growing up. He could still remember the day in school when he first learned that a comet may have been responsible for their end, and for the upheavals that resulted in Man's dominance on Earth.

As glad as he was to be alive, and to be himself, he'd always mourned the passing of the great creatures—and had, since that day, carried a great passion, born of dismay, curiosity, and wonder, for comets.

So when this mission came up, the first mission ever to attempt to match orbits with a comet and gather samples, he fought for a place. Which brought him once more into the depths of space, and the blackness he thought of more and more as his natural home.

4

December 23, 2011

I suppose I wouldn't have gone out at all that night if I hadn't read the obituary section of *The Washington Post*. Four suicides, two men, two women, all under the age of forty-five.

Of course, this was not unexpected news, since Christmas was two days away. The suicide rate usually soars over the holidays in big cities.

So I went out looking for a little frivolity, a little human warmth. Which meant a woman, of course.

In the age of AIDS, I'm as careful as I can be without becoming a hermit.

That night, I needn't have worried.

Because we practiced safe sex, all right, just about the safest you could have.

I slept on the couch with the little red blanket my cat, Tasha, usually takes, and the lady—

her name was Denise and she was some kind of computer expert in the Defense Department—took my bed with the nice warm electric blanket.

The thing was, Denise was brokenhearted. Four weeks ago, over her lunch hour, she'd driven out to deliver a surprise birthday present to her fiancé's apartment. But Denise was the one who got surprised. When she used her key and let herself in, she found him making earnest love to one of the secretaries from his law office.

Which was an eerie parallel to an experience I'd had not long ago, an experience that at least temporarily had shut down the only talent I'd ever possessed.

But, anyway, Denise.

Between crying jags in the bar—we were in the back in a booth so that kind of thing was permissible—we learned that we shared an affinity for Clint Eastwood movies, John O'Hara novels, Vivaldi, Bugs Bunny and Yosemite Sam, and the chocolate cake at the Encore Café over by the Kennedy Center.

When we weren't talking about our interests and passions, we were talking about Rick the lawyer and what a shit he was, and indeed he was.

Then it was closing time and the lights came up in that dreary last-call way they have of doing, and she said, "Have you ever been heart-broken?"

I smiled sadly. "Not past tense. Present. I *am* heartbroken."

"You were dumped?"

"Something like that."

"Don't you ever get scared of the night—when you're alone, I mean. I mean, just the concept of *night.*"

She was two glasses of wine past being exactly coherent, but I knew what she was trying to say. Sometimes night stretched vast and frightening in front of you, and you wondered if you'd ever make it till dawn.

"Sorry, folks, we're closing," said a beefy guy, picking up our wine glasses.

We went outside. She had her arm around my waist and her clean dark hair in my face. She smelled warm and womanly and erotic.

"God, I don't want to leave you," she said. "But I'm not up for sleeping with anybody yet, either."

"I could use a little company myself. C'mon."

"But where—"

"Are you mad?" she had called an hour later from the bedroom.

"No. I'm asleep."

"I'll sleep with you if you really want me to."

"Boy, try and control your enthusiasm, will you?"

"I'm sorry I talked so much about Rick tonight."

She was sobering up and felt embarrassed and probably even a little scared. We had kissed a few times, and then she had guided my hand to one of her sweet little breasts and then just as quickly guided it away, and started sobbing about Rick again.

And so, realizing that I would have to be a noble bastard even if I didn't want to, I had stood her up and walked her into the bedroom, laid her down, and then turned on the electric blanket.

"You need some sleep," I said. "And so do I."

I went out to the kitchen and made myself a cup of tea and then sat up on my bed on the couch and watched the second half of *Winchester '73*, which is one of those old Jimmy Stewart Westerns that gets better, and more morally ambiguous, with each viewing.

After a while, I tiptoed to the bedroom door, opened it, and peeked inside.

For a slight woman of five-feet-four, she made a hell of a lot of noise snoring. But it was sweet, her snoring, and for the first time since climbing the stairs to my apartment door, I was glad she was here. On a snowy night like this, it was just good to know that somebody else was in my apartment.

I went back to the movie and it was about twenty minutes later that she woke up and called out was I mad and I said no I was asleep.

"Maybe I should go home."

"Don't be silly. We're snowed in. Now go back to sleep."

"Really? You aren't mad?"

"Really, I'm not mad."

"You know what I forgot to ask you?" she said.

"What's that?"

"What you do. For a living I mean."

"I'm a freak."

"You're a what?"

I sighed. Actually, that's both what I was *and* what I did for a living. But one thing I'd had to agree to when I'd signed on with the Lab was that I would never divulge what I did. Never. To anybody. And since the federal government was at least marginally the Lab's sponsor, I had to honor my word.

"I do phone surveys."

"Oh." She tried very hard to keep the disappointment from her voice, but she couldn't quite manage it. "You mean sort of like call people on the phone and ask them real irritating questions?"

I smiled. "I must've called you before."

She laughed. "God, don't people swear at you a lot?"

"How much is a lot?"

She laughed again. "Boy, you're really what I needed tonight. You really are. I just wish you were getting something out of it."

"I am getting something out of it. You're a very appealing woman."

"I'd offer to make you breakfast tomorrow, but I'm a terrible cook."

"Tomorrow's Saturday. We can sleep late and then go find a restaurant somewhere."

"G'night."

"Night."

I turned the TV off, and the lights, then lay down and watched the flurries touch the windows, and listened to the snowplows work furiously in the distance. There was something melancholy about it all, but it was not an unpleasant melancholy, and then at last I slept.

5

I've never been much of a sleeper. The people at the Lab explained why to me once— something having to do with certain brain function irregularities—and so the slightest noise wakes me up. The footsteps in the vestibule downstairs woke me up.

I lay for long moments in that limbo of shadow and chill and growing body awareness— the knee that needed scratching, the bladder that needed emptying—and then I focused on the footsteps, wondering who it was, and why they were here. It was late, and mine was the only apartment on the second floor.

Up until a few months ago, I would have had a photograph of my caller by now. Of all the dozens of espers who have passed through the Lab, I was always in the upper three percent for creating the quickest and most detailed mental photographs. We used to practice with portable steel walls. I'd sit on a chair on one side of the wall, and then Dr. Broder would bring somebody into the room and put him on the other side of the wall. Dr. Broder would then ask me to describe this person in detail. I not only gave him color of hair, eyes and necktie; I also gave him warts, moles, and birthmarks.

At the top of the stairs, the footsteps stopped.

I squeezed my eyes shut and concentrated on the darkness that now enveloped me. Used to be so damned easy to conjure up a photograph. I strained to the point that I could feel sweat start to bead on my forehead and a headache begin to pound in both temples.

Footsteps again. Faster now. Had to be a woman. Not heavy enough to make the ancient wooden floor do much more than squeak faintly. A man's weight would have been much noisier.

She paused at the door. Then something nudged the door faintly.

Footsteps again but this time going away.

Down the hall, down the stairs, through the vestibule, out the front door. Quickly. Quickly.

I eased out from beneath the covers, trying not to wake Tasha, who slept at my feet, and walked softly over to the door.

I looked both ways, after I got the door opened, just in case she'd managed to fake me out and was actually hiding nearby with a gun.

But there was nobody. Just a window-rattling blast of cold wind and the dying groans of a house that had lived past its time.

At my feet, however, sitting there on the scuffed yellow linoleum that was probably older than I was, was a fashionable box from Laura Ashley, the trendy Georgetown store that seemed to bedazzle women of all ages.

But why would somebody leave me a Laura Ashley box? Maybe a previous life I'd been a cross-dresser, but in this one I liked being a guy just fine.

I went inside and took it over to the table and set it down and got a good light on it and then lifted the top off.

There was a newspaper clipping inside, dated some six months ago.

ASTRONAUTS TO RETURN
Touchdown Scheduled for Saturday

The joint NASA-EEC comet investigation mission, led by Captain Jack Campbell, is due to touch down at Cape Canaveral at 4:05 AM EST tomorrow. Early press releases heralded the mission as a success, but lately NASA has been uncharacteristically quiet.

Reporters have not been invited to witness the return.

There was a note scrawled on the clipping in red ballpoint. "They never came back," it said. It looked like a woman's handwriting, but I didn't recognize it.

I had known Cap'n Jack. Several years ago, we had done some work together. He was a nice guy, and I'd liked him a lot.

I thought back to the event. I remembered hearing about the comet mission and thinking that it was a great idea, but I couldn't remember how it ended. It seemed that it had sort of vanished in the usual noise of violence and earthquakes and wars and crime that had all somehow, without our ever quite realizing how it happened, become our way of life.

I wondered what had happened to Cap'n Jack, and who had brought me this clipping in such an unusual fashion.

As I thought, I automatically reached out with my mind, sensing for whatever clues could be found within the paper in my hands. There wasn't much, just a faint sensation of fear, and something that may have been pain. That was all, but it was enough to make me even more curious.

I sat up thinking until I heard the first chink of tire chains on the milk trucks of the D.C.

morning. And then the rumble and tumble of people trekking off through the chill gray morning to chill gray jobs.

I ended up sitting up on the couch with Tasha in my lap, fitful sleep taking me down ten minutes at a time.

6

We had breakfast at a bagel place called Maxie's, which on its lunch and dinner menus has the best vegetarian chili ever made. You wouldn't expect to find vegetarian dishes like that on the edge of the inner city, but Maxie's seems to do just fine, partly because some of the more upwardly mobile people who don't have much money are returning to neighborhoods like these and buying fixer-up housing and making affordable homes for themselves and their families. These are the people who watch all the TV shows about health and learn about the remarkable medicinal values of granola and tree bark.

It was a bright and beautiful winter day, and everybody coming through the door looked alert and apple-cheeked healthy, having just finished building snowmen, tossing snowballs at each other, and shooting down sidewalks on their sleds. The scents of coffee and hot apple cider and melting butter were on the air, and Maxie had his Easy Listening station on, the song at this particular moment being Bing Crosby's "White Christmas," and corny as it was, I was glad to hear it again.

"You look tired."

"That's the nicest thing anybody's said to me in a week," I said. And then I grinned. She looked on the edge of crying. Apparently she thought she'd deeply upset me. "Hey, I was kidding. Relax and enjoy yourself."

"I think my period's starting."

"You could still relax and enjoy yourself."

"Have you ever had a period?"

"Maybe in a past life."

She sighed, and then suddenly laughed. "God, the date from hell."

"Would that be me or you?"

"Me, of course." She had a great kid-sister grin and I liked the hell out of her for it. "First all I do is talk about how this guy dumped me, then I take your bed away from you, and then over breakfast I start talking about my period."

"I knew my dream girl would come along if I'd just be patient."

"Would you be willing to try again?"

"Another date, you mean?"

She nodded.

"Sure."

"Really?"

"Really. You're a nice woman. Why wouldn't I?"

She took a bite of her bagel, sipped a little coffee, and then looked to the front door where a dad, mom, and two little girls were all stamping snow from their feet.

"This is my favorite time of year," Denise said. "The snow covers everything. All the dirt, all the violence. Washington's more like a small town then."

"You come from a small town?"

"Gladbrook, Iowa. Is that small enough for you?"

"Did you have running water?"

The kid-sister grin again. "So what was in the Laura Ashley box? That's another thing about me. I'm nosy."

"How'd you find out about the Laura Ashley box?"

"I tiptoed out and went to the bathroom. You had the box on your knees and were staring inside. You looked real intense."

I decided to tell her at least part of the truth. "I don't know what's in the box."

"Really?"

"Really."

"I mean, it wasn't a shirt or a pair of pants or anything. I thought it was a gift from an admirer."

"No such luck," I said.

Denise stared at me for a long moment. "You're serious, aren't you? You really don't know what it is, do you?"

"Maybe we should go back to talking about Rick."

She laughed again. "Now I know you really want to change the subject."

"How's the bagel?"

"You really won't talk about what's in the box anymore?"

This time, I did the grinning. "I really really won't. You say 'really' a lot, you know that? Now finish your bagel."

She finished her bagel and then her coffee and then stood up and said, "I've got to do a load of laundry today so I'd better get going."

"I'll give you a ride."

"There's a Metro stop two blocks from here. Why don't you just walk me over there?"

So I walked her over to the Metro stop. She was right about the snow. It made even this section of the city, not exactly an area of posh high-rises and luxurious condos, look pretty. Sunlight sparkled off ice that seemed more beautiful than the brightest gem; and small black children in pink and buff, blue and red snowsuits looked every bit as healthy and happy and safe as their white suburban counterparts.

If I weren't careful, I'd break into a chorus of "White Christmas" myself.

About half a block from the Metro stop, she slid her red-mittened hand into mine and it made me feel ridiculously good about her and about myself.

Her bus was there right away, even its fumes smelling pleasant on this most gorgeous of winter morns.

Just before she got on, I pulled her close and said, "I really want to see you again, Denise."

"You say it, too."

"Huh?"

" 'Really.' "

"Oh. Yeah. Guess I do."

The driver beeped. "Guess I'd better go," she said.

"Yeah."

"Maybe sometime you'll tell me what's in that box you got."

I smiled. "Soon as I figure it out, I'll let you know."

"Well," she said.

I kissed her and then watched her step up into the bus and start depositing her fare.

As things turned out, I was glad I kissed her because it was the last time I'd ever see her alive.

7

On Fridays, there's always a check waiting for me in a discreet gray envelope in the middle drawer of the desk they've assigned me down at the University where I work. Ostensibly, I'm a research assistant; more accurately, I'm a guinea pig. I let the researchers there poke and prod at me and try to gain a handle on my abilities, and for that they pay me subsistence wages—and agree to keep my name out of any material they publish.

But that's not where the little gray envelope comes from. That's something else entirely. That's a gift from the federal government, for services rendered when I was just a kid.

Back in the '80s, when the serious crime rate was starting to triple, when something as simple as a trip to the corner grocery store became a perilous undertaking, the CIA recruited one hundred "psychically gifted" high school students and began putting them through an experimental program called Vanguard, which was housed in the Broder Labs, Inc., building, a company the CIA had bought years earlier and now used as a front.

We lived in a large dormitory over in Maryland and were bused to Broder every day. In addition to regular schoolwork, we were also tested every day on one of three parapsychological skills—telepathy, clairvoyance, and precognition.

At the time, the Russians dominated the field of serious parapsychology. They had produced at least three students in a program not unlike Vanguard who had stunned everybody who saw them. Unfortunately, all three were killed in a mysterious plane crash over the Ukraine. Some believe they were murdered; others believe that one of the three had developed a subconscious suicide impulse and caused the crash to happen.

The suicide theory isn't as unlikely as it might seem. By 1987, there were only ten people left in Vanguard. More than twenty of the original students had committed suicide; a dozen or so others developed various problems that put them into mental hospitals, some of them permanently. And some lost their esper skills entirely. There's long been a theory, chiefly among the Russians, that the most psychically gifted human beings are children. The

Russians insist that as we grow older, we lose our innate skills. And to some degree, they've been able to chart this, which is where Vanguard came in. The CIA wanted to create a small corps of para-law enforcement officers who could use their psi powers to stop crime—infiltrate mob organizations, track down especially violent murderers, help police during interrogations to determine the guilt or innocence of a suspect. It was believed that if you trained high-school-age people to become comfortable with their skills, and to practice those skills on a regular basis, you wouldn't have the falling off the Russians had noted. They would go on to maintain their skills over their lifetimes. Well, we were now down to ten percent, suicide, mental problems, and fading skills having taken their toll. The people who ran Vanguard were now searching genetics for various answers, but as yet the biochemical and physiological study of espers had yielded very little.

Not that there wasn't a solution, if you were willing to pay the price: an experimental drug called sorahein. While the feds are never eager to talk about it, sorahein was given to several older members of our group, members whose esper powers had begun to wane. The upside was fantastic—greatly increased ability to scan and probe, even new abilities such as psychokinesis. The downside was just as fantastic—

terrible psychotic episodes, "like the worst bad acid trips of the sixties only a thousand times worse," as one of the participants described it to me. Hence, the murder rate, several of the people killing their mates; hence, the suicide rate, several of the people killing themselves. The trick, it was said, was to survive the first hour. It was recommended that for this period you lock yourself in a room with a trusted friend, sort of like an acid guide from hippie days, and have him or her restrain you from doing anything terribly foolish. If your heart didn't explode, or if you weren't mentally maimed in some permanent way, then you most likely emerged from that hour with enormously enhanced esper powers. The trouble was, the effects of sorahein didn't last very long.

By the mid-nineties, the project had been disbanded, the Lab shut down. Those of us who were still sane were released, with oaths of secrecy and national security sealing our lips and weekly checks to reward us. They kept tabs on us, brought us in occasionally for exams and tests. They'd even helped the people here at the University get in touch with me.

As for the CIA itself, I never did learn what they did with the information they gained from us, but I had my suspicions. Every once in a while, I'd see an item in the papers, an inexplicable death or a case cracked by information that seemed to come from nowhere, and I'd wonder.

But I wasn't involved any longer, and that was enough for me.

These days I was having a few problems with my own skills. I was doing very badly on my weekly Zenner card test—trying to guess the number on the far side of the card they were holding up. The University people had shipped me up to the Princeton Anomalies Research Laboratory to test some of my basic skills on their state-of-the-art equipment . . . and found my scores to be definitely in decline.

If I ran true to pattern, my skills would give out entirely in the next twelve to eighteen months, and then, at age forty-three, I'd find myself with a nice little government pension and a lot of great business opportunities in the Amway organization.

I would have to become an ordinary citizen, one with no special powers at his command, and that wasn't a pleasant prospect at all. Not when you'd been a member of a chosen elite for so many years. For this reason, I carried a small vial of sorahein with me constantly—just in case I needed to give it a try.

I slipped the gray envelope into my coat pocket, not even bothering to try to get a "read" from it. I'd done that once, years ago, just for kicks, aiming for some kind of impression of the person who'd put it in my drawer. I'd gotten nothing—and this was back when my powers were at their peak—so I'd tried it again. And again. And again. Not once did I receive a single impression, no matter how fleeting.

And that scared me. Not because of what it said about my powers, but because of what it said about theirs. Either the entire process was automated, without a single human hand ever touching either my check or the envelope, or they had come up with a way to hide their psychic fingerprints. Either way, it was a prospect I didn't like to think about.

Also in that center drawer, right next to where the envelope had lain, was a small brown bottle of pills. It was unlabeled, as always, but I knew what it was: another little aspect of our agreement. The bottle held a week's supply of vitamins, specially prepared to help maintain esper powers, and I had to take them if I wanted to keep receiving those little gray envelopes.

I unscrewed the cap, shook two of the unmarked gelatin capsules into my palm, swallowed them dry, and put the bottle in my other coat pocket. Then I closed the drawer and locked it once more—for all the good it would do.

* * *

Except for the cleaning crew, the Lab was empty, everybody having gone home for the holiday.

I went to the back of the Lab, to the library, six thousand scientific books in all, and I ignored every last one of them. What I wanted was the computer terminal on the table up against the far wall. It was connected to dozens of major databases, and through the Internet to hundreds more. I wanted to see what it could tell me.

I sat down in front of it, powered it up, logged on, and started searching through all the news services for information about the comet exploration mission.

I found nothing. At least, nothing helpful. There were mentions of it in the months prior to launch; there were updates as it neared the comet; and there were even two brief reports stating, basically, that it had reached its goal. And that was it. Not one additional mention anywhere. I couldn't even find the paper that had run the clipping I'd found in the Laura Ashley box.

I sat back in my chair, puzzled and deeply disturbed. Something was going on, and somebody wanted me to know about it. But what, and who, and why?

There were no more answers to be found there. I closed up, locked up, and left. My envelope, my pills, and my clipping all snug in my pockets, I trundled down the block to the Metro stop where I froze my balls off for the next twenty minutes while Perry Como holiday records blared from a speaker on top of an appliance store across the street.

Long blue shadows were about to bring night rushing in, and the melancholy was back on me again. I was just enough like my psychic brothers and sisters to understand why so many of them had killed themselves.

8

The neighborhood looked pretty at dusk, blue and red and green holiday lights strung across windows and doors, and Christmas music on the air, tiny tots finishing up their snowmen in the rich blue shadows of an early winter night.

I stopped at the corner grocery, where it always smells of cold cuts and onions, and bought a quart of beer and a loaf of wheat bread and a copy of *Time*, and then went on home.

As I was inserting my key, I heard Tasha crying inside my apartment. She gets lonely when I'm gone and tells me about it when I get back.

As soon as I opened the door, I knew something was wrong.

For one thing, the light was on in the tiny kitchenette area. I could see a big bowl of spaghetti on the counter and a pan of sauce, presumably for the spaghetti, simmering on the burner. The place smelled homier and friendlier than it ever had.

Somebody was making me dinner. My money was on Denise, who had probably gotten the old Slav who runs the place to let her into my apartment.

The second thing I noticed was that the place had been very hastily picked up but still bore signs of having been searched frantically. The throw pillows on the couch were not in the right position, and the desk over in the corner had been cleaned off impeccably. It had never in its history been cleaned off impeccably.

Flashes—images—mental pictures tried to come into focus. For the children of Vanguard, emotions have colors. Danger is always an ominous red. Even though I wasn't getting any clear images—perhaps my powers really were fading in a permanent way—a red mist was rolling in front of my eyes.

Somebody was in my apartment. I groped on the desk for my large black flashlight, large enough to be useful as a club. Then I slipped the Walther PPK out of its holster.

Danger. Rolling misty red.

I took three steps into the deep shadows of the apartment and that was when my foot nudged against Denise's ankle.

I clicked on the flashlight and played the beam over her face and body. They'd tortured her. Her beautiful, aristocratic nose had been broken and her tender blue eyes had been viciously blackened. From the bruises on her neck, I assumed she'd been strangled. As for the rest, I tried not to look too closely. Her skirt and panties had been ripped away and there was some evidence of mutilation, an art practiced by self-respecting sexual psychopaths around the world.

I looked over at Tasha, who sat on the middle pillow of the couch, watching me curiously.

I learned a long time ago that there are no heroes in street fights. There's just the guy who delivers the most violence first.

And then I saw him. Not a strong image but enough to identify him as chunky, wearing a black topcoat, a black fedora, and black gloves cinched tight on the hands that had murdered Denise.

Somewhere in the apartment.

Right now.

The image vanished, leaving me standing there with my pistol. The bedroom. It was the only place he could possibly be.

I looked down at Denise again. I wanted to keep her bloodied face in my mind. It would give me some extra power when I confronted him.

I went through the bedroom doorway as if I

had no suspicion whatsoever that he was hiding behind the door.

He did just what I hoped he'd do.

When I was four or five steps into the bedroom, he lunged at me, but I was ready for him. I turned and swung the butt of my pistol and felt a satisfying crunch as it cracked against his left shoulder.

My psychic image had been exactly right—beefy guy, dressed in black. The only thing the image had failed to convey was the tiny spray can he was just now bringing up in his gloved left hand. He leaned a little bit forward, just as I was starting to swing again, and sprayed me directly in the face with some kind of chill crystal mist.

Denise was dead. The newspaper clipping was folded carelessly in my pocket. I had just been treated to some kind of chemical formulation that was shutting down all my senses at once.

Darkness.

Deep rolling cold darkness.

I heard myself hit the floor, and then I heard nothing at all.

9

December 3

Seeing the stars like this, through a thin viewport instead of a thick atmosphere, had always been Wendy's favorite part of being an astronaut. There was a feeling that came with stargazing, a sense of majesty, of beauty, of awe, that she'd never found on Earth. Now, though, not even that sight could distract her from her worries.

There was something wrong with Colonel Jacobs, but Wendy couldn't figure out what it was. Susan Jacobs was the other American on board, and she was the commander of this mission. Wendy had never flown with her before, and had only met her a few times, but all the active members of NASA's elite astronaut program were well known, and Colonel Jacobs was definitely acting out of character.

It was nothing big, nothing like taking unnecessary risks or giving confusing orders. Instead, it was a lot of little things. Like that good luck kiss she'd given all the male astronauts before they left. That was not a NASA tradition, and Wendy had never heard of Colonel Jacobs doing that before.

By itself, it didn't mean anything, but taken together with all the other little things . . . well, Wendy didn't know what it meant. But there was definitely something wrong with Colonel Jacobs.

"Hey, Abronowitz. How's it going?" Miriam Goldmann, the other woman on board, was just coming out of the hatchway into the little service compartment where Wendy was working.

"Okay. I should have this last suit finished in another ten minutes or so."

Wendy was examining each of the crew members' space suits. They had all been checked and rechecked several times back on Earth, but it was customary to do it throughout a mission as well. You never knew when you might need one, and a cracked seal could spell a slow and painful death.

"Need any help?" Goldmann was Israeli. She'd been born and raised in the Occupied Territories, but spoke English like a native.

"No, thanks. I'm about finished." Wendy could have added that she was using this busy work to keep her mind off Colonel Jacobs, but she wasn't sure she wanted to bring that up.

A minute later, though, Miriam did it for her.

"Say, Abronowitz, you notice anything weird about this mission?"

Wendy nodded. "Yeah, a few things. What about you?"

"A few things. You notice that Jacobs seems a bit distracted? I swear, there are times when I think she's receiving radio signals through her fillings. The way she just sits there staring off into space can be kind of unnerving, you know?"

Wendy gave a quick, guilty glance out the viewport to her right, but she nodded. She knew just what Goldmann meant.

"And what about that rash?" she asked. All the men had come down with it at the same time, about three weeks into the mission. It was a minor thing, hardly itched at all, but it was odd. The three of them got it in the same place, their inner forearms, and they all had it for the same length of time. Wendy was no doctor, but it had seemed to her to be reminiscent of Lyme disease—which just wasn't something you picked up on a NASA flight.

Miriam nodded. "Not like any space sickness I've ever seen, that's for sure." She hesitated, then asked, "Say, Abronowitz, you notice anything odd about the lighting in here?"

Wendy frowned. "What do you mean?"

"Well, this'll sound kind of odd, but there've been times when I swear I saw these orange reflections in the eyes of Jacobs and the others. You see anything like that?"

Wendy shook her head. "No, but then I haven't been looking. I'll keep a watch out for it from now on."

Miriam nodded, and started to say something else, but then they both heard someone coming up through the hatchway and she fell silent. A moment later, Colonel Jacobs stuck her head out.

"Those suits about finished, Abronowitz?" she asked.

Wendy nodded. "Five more minutes."

"Good, 'cause you've got an EVA in fifteen. Get yourself together and report when you're ready."

She gave Goldmann a long, searching stare, then withdrew.

A space walk, Wendy thought. That wasn't scheduled. What in the world was going on?

10

"You're asking me if I killed her, aren't you?"

"I suppose I am, yes."

"Well, I didn't."

"You just came in here—"

"—and found her just where she was when you got here. And then somebody—"

"—sprayed something in your face—"

"—and knocked me out."

Her name was Reston, she was a D.C. Homicide Inspector, and you doted on her blue, blue eyes and pretty smile at your peril. She was all business, and her particular business happened to be murder. Oh, yes: she was a past master at mocking you with your own words.

"You met Denise last night?"

"Yes. Just as I said."

"And you came back here."

"Right."

"And she slept in your bed and you slept on the couch."

"Correct."

"Do you know what that sounds like to me?"

I sighed. "I suppose it sounds like we had some sort of argument."

"But you didn't."

"Right. We didn't."

"She didn't reject your sexual advances?"

"There weren't any sexual advances."

"You meet a woman in a bar, a kind of pickup bar if you will, Mr. Raines, and you bring her back to your apartment and you don't make any sexual advances?"

"She was depressed about a love affair."

"Ah. And being the civilized man you are, you kept your hands to yourself."

"Exactly."

"I don't believe you, Mr. Raines. I don't believe you at all."

We sat at the rickety table in the living room and looked down at the street. In the soft streetlight glow, you could see snow flurries again. The fat snowmen looked lonely now, and the silver angels in the cracked and taped windows looked sad.

In the old days, when my abilities were functioning at full strength, I would have peeped Inspector Patricia Reston and found out what was really in her mind.

But I didn't need to. She'd already made it quite clear that she was going to do what too many homicide detectives do, find a suspect and direct the entire investigation toward him, without ever once considering any other suspects. It's not a frame-up exactly, just very lazy police work.

The ambulance men lifted Denise into the body bag. The zipper's noise was unnaturally loud, oppressively gross.

The other ten people—some with cameras, some with fingerprint kits, three or four with handfuls of small plastic bags which they were constantly filling with things from couch and floor and kitchen—all kept busy. Every once in a while, when Inspector Reston got off an especially nasty remark, they'd look at each other and grin and wink.

Apparently, the good Inspector had something of a rep with her peer group.

The overhead lights were on in all the rooms. I'd never realized before how old and shabby this place really was. It was like looking in a mirror on some gray hangover morning and realizing suddenly that you'd become old and infirm. Then I saw that somebody had brushed against my little silver Christmas tree, the one Denise had said was so depressing, and knocked it to the floor and stepped on it. This would be a night for the memory book.

"Say for the sake of argument that I buy your story, Mr. Raines. You know, that somebody broke in here and tortured Denise because they were looking for something."

"That's what happened."

"All right, then, what were they looking for?"

I started to tell her, but I realized how silly it would all sound.

There's this newspaper clipping, a story that's been removed from the news services, that somebody left outside my door last night in a Laura Ashley box.

"I don't know."

"Somebody breaks in and tortures a woman and kills her, but you don't have any idea what they'd be looking for?"

"I'm afraid that's true."

"You're a pip, Mr. Raines. You really are. And you know what?"

"What?"

"I'm going to enjoy taking you down for questioning. I really am. Because I don't even like to think of how much that woman must have suffered in the last few hours of her life."

"I need to make a phone call."

"You going to order in a pizza?"

This brought a couple of chuckles from her friends, a few of whom had just made the trek up the stairs, bringing with them the hard clean scent of fresh air. I wanted to be out in that fresh air, in the cold clean snow, and walking away from all this, from all memory of how poor

Denise looked after the killer had finished with
her, and the memory of that newspaper clipping
in the Laura Ashley box.

I stood up. "All right?"

She stood up. "I suppose it's all right, Mr.
Raines."

"I'd like to use the bedroom and close the
door."

She thought a moment. "Bob, clear the bedroom for a minute, then you stand at the door
while Mr. Raines makes a phone call."

She straightened her gray Georgio Armani
suit, always aware of her looks and their effect
on men.

"You have three minutes, Mr. Raines."

I went into the bedroom, trying not to look at
the blood streaks on wall and sheets.

I had to call three numbers before I found
him. Even though he was very high up in the
CIA, he lived in Georgetown and was a social-
ite of sorts. Some nights, he'd once told me,
he'd hit as many as six different parties. I could
only hope that, after all these years, he'd still
remember me and still want to help.

I talked. I talked fast and I talked a little desperate. He wasn't the reassuring type. He didn't
stroke me, he didn't console me, he simply said,
right at the end, a whoop of champagne laughter exploding behind him, "I'll take care of it,"
and hung up.

I went back to the living room.

Inspector Reston was looking down at the street. "This isn't going to be a very nice Christmas for Denise's folks."

"No," I said, "it isn't."

"That's the worst part of this whole job. Even worse than looking at mutilated bodies. Calling the parents or the spouses." She slowly raised her head and studied me. "You have a nice face. Not handsome, really, but intelligent and sensitive in a masculine sort of way." Then a cold smile curved her lips. "That's what everybody will say when they see you on TV, Mr. Raines. He's got such a nice, warm face. How could he have tortured that woman that way?"

"I didn't kill her."

"Of course you did, Mr. Raines, and pretty soon you'll drop all the bullshit and tell me you did, and then we can get down to wrapping this case up."

The phone rang. One of her detectives got it, said something inaudible into the receiver, and then said, "Inspector, it's for you."

The cold smile again. "Don't go anywhere, Mr. Raines."

She went over to the phone, put the receiver to ear and mouth, and said, "Inspector Reston," and then said nothing else for perhaps two minutes.

Then: "This is horseshit. Do you know that, Commissioner? Really horseshit."

She was silent again, this time for maybe a full minute. Listening. And rolling her eyes the entire time.

And then she managed to whisper a good-bye that conveyed great defiance. That's not easy to do in a whisper.

She walked back over to me. "You didn't tell me you had friends, Mr. Raines."

"Everybody has friends."

"Not friends with a capital F."

"I really didn't kill her."

"Of course not, Mr. Raines. How could a fine fellow like you ever do anything like that?" She frowned. "I have friends, too, Mr. Raines. Capital F friends. And I'm going to spend all day tomorrow having them call your friends and convince them that they're impeding a murder investigation." The nasty smile. "Enjoy your freedom, Mr. Raines. You won't have it much longer."

To her cohorts she said, "Wrap things up here. I'm going back to the station."

And then she was gone, snatching her blue winter coat from the closet on her way out.

One of the cops said, "She's a pisser, isn't she?"

I nodded. "Uh-huh."

"Her son was killed last summer on his bike. She hasn't adjusted to it yet, I don't think."

I felt sorry for her, of course, her son killed and all, but I resented feeling sorry for her. The last person I wanted to see as a real human being was that icy bitch Inspector Patricia Reston of the D.C. police. People are a lot easier to hate when you don't have to see them as human.

11

There was a time in my life, and not so long ago either, when my Walther PPK was my best friend. I had gone through a period where I felt I had to give something back, something more than I was doing at the Lab, and so I offered my services as a consultant to the U.S. government. I ended up with the Drug Enforcement Agency which, in turn, loaned me to a group of drug cowboys who theoretically answered to the Justice Department. We spent four months in various Caribbean countries trying to set up a major dealer who also happened to be the CEO of a Fortune 500 company. Two nights before it all went down, I was able to get a mindlock on the CEO and know exactly where and when he'd be so we could carry out the raid. You have to understand, a pure mindlock is rare. A lot of variables have to be just right before it's possible. But I lucked out, and we nailed the CEO with very little trouble. The problem was, on the plane back to the States, I started to doze off, at which point I always start to pick up free-floating mental information from a lot of the people around me, something I would compare to dialing around on a radio. One piece of information was especially interesting. Friends of the CEO had bought off one of the cowboys, and he was about to hijack the plane and turn it back to the sheltering palms of the CEO's mansion. I picked this information up just as the cowboy was starting to draw his Magnum. And that was when I drew my Walther. The DEA folks still talk about "the shoot-out at 40,000 feet." Actually, it wasn't much of a thing at all, just two well-trained marksmen drawing down on each other. I was luckier than he was; true, one of his dum-dum bullets took off a substantial chunk of my right shoulder; but my dum-dum bullet took an even more substantial chunk of his right lung and heart.

Now, as I stood on the dark, wintry expanse of Princess Street in Alexandria, I thought of the shoot-out and that night so many years ago, and you know the funny thing? I still got scared, my heart rate increasing, a fine sheen of sweating covering my face and armpits, and even a barely perceptible tic in my left eye. I had no illusions about myself. I was a telepath—at least I was when all my talents were working—not a hero. But despite that, or perhaps because of it, I took my Walther with me everywhere.

Nothing was going on in the well-kept brick Tudor that looked so snug and cozy in the winter silver moonlight. The sales slip in the Laura Ashley box had led me here. Had the receipt been left in the box by accident, or was it some sort of coincidence?

I looked up and down the street, a block of Volvos and Saabs and BMWs, with the occasional Jag for spice. Upper-echelon bureaucrats, no doubt, given the address. The lights were off in most houses. The late shows were done for the night, and alarm clocks would be going off soon enough. Had to pay for those cars somehow.

Five minutes later, the car came tearing down the street, far too fast for the icy surface. It was a black BMW and it came to a sliding halt in front of me.

The automatic window on the passenger side worked downward. I looked inside at a very attractive red-haired woman in her forties. She wore a London Fog trench coat and a snug pair of black leather gloves. One of her hands held a formidable Magnum, which was pointed directly at my chest.

"Get in," she said.

I tried for a fast scan, but they usually don't work very well and this one didn't work at all. I picked up a cloud of fear and panic in the lady, but you hardly had to be a telepath to deduce that.

I got in.

Cigarette smoke was heavy and blue on the air.

I looked in the dash ashtray, where a half-smoked filter tip sent up curling wraiths of smoke.

She followed my gaze and said, "Oh, God, you're not going to give me an antismoking sermon, are you?"

I smiled. "Not while you're holding the gun on me."

"Oh, shit," she said, glancing in her rearview. "Look."

A big, shiny black American car—a Lincoln I guessed—was shooting down the street directly at us. I might have tried to tell her that she should relax, that they weren't necessarily interested in us, but then their gunfire told me otherwise. Two crisp bullets on the cold midnight air, two nights before Christmas.

And then we were off.

You know from car chases. God knows you've seen enough TV and movies to know how car chases work.

You go up and down dark, narrow streets, the chase car catching up here and there, close enough for the guy riding shotgun to squeeze off a few shots anyway, and then the lead car pulling away for a time, skidding around impossible corners and still managing to stay upright, and then hitting speeds of one hundred or better on the straightaways.

It went on for twenty, twenty-five minutes, and by the time I convinced her to let me out of the car, we were in an alley near the boyhood home of Robert E. Lee (that's how they describe it on all the maps, anyway) and I was standing in the shadow of a huge elm tree that was very black against the silver glow of the moon.

The Lincoln was approximately a block away. I heard it before I saw it. They'd temporarily lost us, and I'd decided to take advantage of it.

I crouched, Walther in hand, ready to jump into the street and surprise them.

And surprise them I did.

When they were several yards away from the elm, traveling at maybe eighty, eight-five miles an hour, I stepped into the street and opened fire.

The first thing I shot out was their windshield.

The second thing I shot out was their rear tire.

They had been so focused on finding her car that I doubt they even saw me in the last moments of their lives.

The Lincoln, skidding and fishtailing, ran up

over a curb down from the alley where the black BMW sat, and rammed into the corner of a building.

I hadn't really wanted them to die, but apparently the gods did because the gas tank went up in a whoosh of flame, and then there was a white flash and an explosion, and then screams, pretty horrible screams, and then there was a second explosion and the night was lit up with a fire that had a kind of ugly beauty.

I stood, transfixed, and watched.

At least the screaming had stopped.

I didn't hear the BMW sneak up, but when I turned around the passenger door was open and she was pointing the Magnum at me again.

"Now we can have our talk, Mr. Raines," she said, as sirens started wailing in the night.

I got in, and we left the fire, and the death, receding behind us.

By the end of the block she was hitting sixty-five.

I sat back and did my best to peep her. She was frantic and confused. About all I could get was that she knew something about the newspaper clipping—and something about astronauts and the President of the United States.

I could have pulled my gun, but I figured I'd learn more if I let her tell me in her own time and her own way.

By now she was hitting eighty.

12

"You're one hell of a driver."

"Thank you," she said. "My father would be glad to hear you say that."

"Your father?"

"He was a test car driver in Detroit. Mostly for Ford. He also raced sports cars. He always wanted a son, but he had to make do with me. I was driving by the time I was ten."

"How old were you when you started smoking?"

She laughed. "God, what are you, some kind of minister or something?"

I shook my head. "No, just somebody who doesn't appreciate secondary smoke laying down a coat of asphalt on his lungs. You've smoked four cigarettes in the last forty-five minutes."

"Maybe I'm nervous."

"Maybe you are. But lung cancer isn't going to help."

We were at a stoplight in residential George-town. Some of the more fancily decorated houses still had their displays lit up in a kind of macho Christmas contest. My house is prettier than yours. That sort of thing. You know, the real spirit of Christmas.

"There. Are you happy?"

"I appreciate it," I said, looking down at the dash ashtray where she'd just ground her filter tip into a dozen pieces of glowing ash.

"Maybe you could roll the window up now? I'm freezing."

"Give it a few minutes. Till the smoke clears."

"You push your wife around like this?"

"I don't have a wife. Not now, anyway."

"That's probably why she isn't around any more. Treatment like this." She sounded mad, but then she smiled. "I probably shouldn't be so insulting. I mean, I haven't even introduced myself."

"Well, I haven't introduced myself, either. But I suspect you know a hell of a lot more about me than I know about you."

"How about some breakfast?"

"Fine," I said.

Breakfast sounded just right.

I had an Egg-Beater cheese omelet, two pieces of toast, a large glass of orange juice, and three cups of coffee.

"Growing boy," she said, sitting across from me in the noisy restaurant. A lot of party goers were staggering around after having way too much holiday cheer. Most of them were likely in training for New Year's Eve. "I wish I could eat like that and stay as thin as you are."

"Genes."

She sighed. "Even with smoking, I weigh ten pounds more than I want to."

"You look great."

"I really wasn't fishing for compliments."

"I know. But I thought I'd just say it. Since it was on my mind anyway."

And she did look great.

Redheaded women have always seemed a mite more seductive than most other women—all other things being equal, of course—and she was no exception. True, she was a bit overweight, but it was a nice kind of overweight. She sat there in her nice tan trench coat and her nice white turtleneck sweater and her nice gold loop earrings and looked fetching indeed. But then I thought of poor Denise, and how she'd never again have a chance to look fetching, and I felt like a shit for being so taken with the woman across from me. I studied her large diamond wedding ring and felt chastened.

She said, "You know my husband."

"Oh?"

"I'm Pam Campbell."

I thought for a minute. "Cap'n Jack? The astronaut?"

She nodded.

"He's still missing, isn't he?" I said.

She stared at me a long moment. She chose not to answer my question. "I know about the Lab."

"Oh?"

"And what you people did there."

I said nothing.

"My husband is mildly telepathic," she said. "Nothing like what you guys can do, of course, but he's always been sensitive to other people's moods, able to tell when someone was lying to him, things like that. Anyway, he's been curious about psi powers since he was a kid, and on one of his first shuttle missions he wanted to try some experiments."

I remembered. Edgar Mitchell had done something similar back in the sixties, on one of the old Mercury missions. He'd asked people all over the world to think of a specific image, and then he tried to see if he could pick that image up in space. It hadn't worked.

Jack and I had a bit more luck. He asked his superiors at NASA how to go about it. They made some inquiries, and one day a guy in a snap brim hat showed up at the Lab. He wanted someone to assist in testing the range of telepathy. I was that someone.

Jack and I met three times before he went into space, to sort of set up a link between us. We did the standard tests, the two of us alternating as sender and receiver, and we logged our scores. Then, while he was in space, we did it again. The really interesting thing was that our scores were the same whether we were ten feet apart or ten thousand miles.

That had been a long time ago, but I still remembered it. It had been an exciting experiment, and Jack was a likable guy. Now here I sat with his wife across from me in a restaurant booth at two in the morning.

"All right, Pam," I said, sipping my coffee. She'd chosen one of those restaurants where they leave you the pot. "Tell me everything."

She sighed, leaned back in her seat, and lit up another cigarette. I didn't say anything, but I found myself wishing that psychokinesis was one of my abilities. It would be handy to be able to just will the smoke away from my lungs.

"You know about the comet mission," she said.

I shook my head. "No. I heard about it, yes, but I wouldn't say I knew about it. Why don't you tell me all about it?"

She blew smoke up toward the ceiling. "It was Jack's dream. You know—or maybe you don't—that he'd retired from active duty. Not his choice, of course; Jack was never one to admit there were things he couldn't do, or to let the idea of his own safety interfere with the job. But this was a rule: no space flights after age forty-five. That is, it was a rule until they discovered this comet, and decided to send a manned mission to investigate it.

"Jack—well, he had an interest in comets, and he called in a few favors on this one. The end result was that he was put in charge of the mission, and guaranteed a seat on the ship." She looked at the coffee cup cooling in front of her. "Damn," she muttered, "I should have picked a place where we could get a drink."

The beleaguered waitress came over and replaced our coffeepot. I'd come from a working class family myself and one year, when I was thirteen, my father had had a serious operation that had laid him up for six months. Like this woman, my mother had worked nights as a waitress. She'd hated it, but she hadn't had much choice. That's why I don't tolerate people who are rude to waitresses. I'm not a big fan of bullies.

I slipped my wallet out, slipped four crisp green ones from inside, and then put them on top of the bill, where I'd already put a twenty.

"That's quite a tip."

"I'm sentimental about waitresses."

She smiled. "You're a strange guy, Mr. Raines."

"So I've been told." I sipped coffee. "Now, you were telling me about the mission."

"It was an eight-week mission. Twenty-five days to get there and match orbits, six days to study it, and twenty-five more to get back. There were six members of the crew; Jack was the captain."

She sipped at her coffee, made a face, and lit up another cigarette. I still didn't make a sound.

"You know, Jack's been on more than a dozen missions, and I was terrified over each one. The things that can go wrong—and the sheer help-lessness if anything does go wrong—well, it's cost me plenty of sleep over the years. This was no different. The first part went fine. We were in constant radio contact, and I was able to talk to Jack a couple of times a day. No privacy, of course, but you get used to that. Then, after they reached the comet, security started tight-ening up. I couldn't talk to Jack as often, or for as long, and then I couldn't talk to him at all. By the time the mission was scheduled to start the trip back, no one at NASA was telling me anything."

She ground her cigarette out, pushed her cof-fee cup aside, and looked me in the eye. "And that, Mr. Raines, is where it's at right now. It's been more than six months, and I still have no idea what's happened. I don't know if my husband is still up with that damn comet, lost somewhere in space, or held prisoner in some government hangar somewhere. I know a lot of people at NASA, believe me; I have quite a few friends there, and no one has been able to tell me a thing."

She reached for her cigarettes and I saw how badly her hand was shaking, and how hard she was trying to keep me from seeing it. I reached out and put my hand on hers.

"It's all right, Pam," I said. "It's all right to be scared. And I promise, I'll do what I can to help."

She gave me a shaky smile and pulled her hand away from the cigarettes. "Thank you," she said.

"There's something you should know, though," I said. "I've been having some problems lately."

"What kind of problems?"

I glanced out the window. Snow flurries filled the air again. People were scraping off their windshields, and cars were fishtailing their way up the sloping driveways. I thought of Denise, then, and felt as sad as Pam had looked a moment ago.

"The Russians have a theory about telepathic power."

"What's their theory?"

"That we lose our powers as we get older. That after sixteen, it's basically downhill."

"You've lost your powers?" Desperation and anger sounded faintly in her voice.

"Not completely. But I'm not functioning at maximum capacity, either. Sort of hit and miss."

She gave me a long, level, measuring look. "I still want you to try."

"Try what, Pam?"

She paused, her eyes still locked with mine, before turning away and pulling her purse off the seat beside her. It was a large tan bag, almost as big as a backpack, and from it she took a framed wall plaque.

"I don't know if you're aware of it, Mr. Raines, but they don't let you wear jewelry into space. Something about the g-forces during liftoff and reentry. Anyway, Jack always leaves his wedding ring behind. It's the only time he ever takes it off." She paused for a moment, and I didn't need my powers to know the depth of feeling she was experiencing right then. "Our twenty-fifth wedding anniversary was in September. I decided to surprise him, so shortly after he left on this mission I took both our rings to a jeweler and had them joined and mounted on this plaque. Sort of a symbol of our lives together, you know? I had bought a new set of rings, and had planned on marrying him all over again on our anniversary."

She put on a brave smile. "Well, I guess maybe we can do that on our next anniversary. Anyway, Mr. Raines, I remembered that you had the ability to receive impressions from objects, and I thought maybe the ring he'd worn for almost twenty-five years would carry enough of him for you to tell me—" Her voice broke off as a sudden swell of emotion overtook her. She blinked and tried again, "For you to tell me—" and again that was as far as she got.

"It's all right, Pam," I said. "I understand."

But she shook her head. "I need you to tell me if he's alive, Mr. Raines, and if he is, I need you to help me find him. Can you do that, Mr. Raines? Will you do that?"

I wanted to reach out for her hand again, but I sensed she didn't want comfort.

I nodded. "If I can, Pam," I said. "I'll help you if I can."

She handed me the plaque. It was the size of a sheet of typing paper turned on its side and had a glass front and a wooden frame. The rings were polished to a high gloss and set on a bed of black satin. Beneath them was a small brass plate with the words, "Jack and Pamela Campbell, September 27, 1986, From two into one, forever."

I turned it over in my hands, but I couldn't see any way to open it up. After a moment, I looked up at Pam.

"I have to be able to touch the rings," I said.

She frowned. "It doesn't open. It's a symbol, you know? Kind of corny, I suppose—"

"I don't think it's corny at all," I said. Which wasn't the truth, but she didn't need to know that. "But I do need to touch the rings for this to work."

She sighed. "Break the glass."

"Pam—"

"Break the glass."

"Pam, this might not work, you know. I'd hate—"

"Break the glass. It's all right. I'd rather have my husband than a symbol. Besides, I can always get it remade."

I nodded, but I handed the plaque back to her. "You break the glass," I said.

She gave me a wan little smile, then set the plaque on the seat beside her. Slipping off one of her shoes—she was wearing flats, not heels—she used it to shatter the glass and clear away the shards. Then she handed it back to me.

"Take it off its mounting if you have to," she said.

I only nodded. Already I was reaching into myself, seeking that place where all my images are born.

Sometimes, when this works, it's like a dream, so smooth and easy; other times, it's work, the images fighting me like the memories of a dream I'm desperately trying to recall. And then there are the times, more common of late, when it simply doesn't work at all.

This time it worked, but it wasn't easy.

I received impressions, not images: pain, darkness, pain, fear, pain, struggle, pain, pain, pain. And there was something else, too, something that in all my years of reading objects and people I'd never encountered, a feeling of something I could only call *alienness*. I didn't know what it was, and I didn't know what it meant, so for the time being I decided not to mention it to Pam.

I opened my eyes and found her staring at me with an intensity that was almost frightening.

"Tell me," she said, her voice under tight control. "Is my husband alive?"

I looked down at my hand, where it was resting lightly on the rings. I had apparently cut myself on a shard of glass she'd missed, because there was a thin film of blood on the shiny yellow gold.

"I think so," I said, and I was surprised to hear how hoarse I sounded. A wave of weakness hit me then, and I realized that, though it had felt as though the encounter had only lasted a few seconds, in reality it had probably taken much longer than that.

"Is he all right?" she asked.

At that, I raised my eyes to hers once again, and gave her the only answer I could. "I don't know," I said. "I honestly don't know."

13

Out in Pam's car, with the engine warming up and the heater on full blast, she turned to me and said, "Are you sure you want to do this now? You seemed pretty tired in there."

I nodded. "Precognition is not normally one of my talents," I said, "but I've got a feeling about this."

"A good feeling, I hope."

"No. The feeling that there's no time to lose."

I had the plaque in my lap. Now, as she put the car into gear and pulled out onto the street, I laid my fingers lightly on the rings and opened myself once more. This time, I was not trying for any specific images; instead, I was hoping for some sense of where Jack was at that moment.

For a long while I got nothing. The heater worked on my feet, thawing them out, but still there was a core of coldness emanating from deep within me.

"Are you all right?" Pam asked.

I looked at her.

"You keep rubbing your shoulder."

I looked down. She was right. I'd been unconsciously massaging my left shoulder. There was a pain there, an ache I'd never felt before.

"An old war wound?" she asked.

"I don't know," I said. Then, "Turn here," I said. "Turn right."

"You're getting something?" she asked as she made the turn.

I nodded. "Something."

It was a tenuous connection. I was receiving no images, no impressions, and yet I felt I knew where he was. Directions came to me as instinct, as though I were traveling a path I'd known as a child. And all the while, the pain in my shoulder continued to build.

We pulled up outside a long, ugly, brick building. It had a wide driveway closed off by a metal gate. There was a guard shack beside the gate, with a light burning inside.

"This is it?" Pam asked.

"This is it."

There was a sign on the stone wall beside the gate. It said: "Hastings House."

"This is a mental asylum," Pam said.

I nodded. "Let's go."

She put the car in gear and pulled up to the gates. When the guard came out, I peeped at him and told her what name to give. He gave us a pair of visitor badges, told Pam where to park, and waved us through.

The snow on the ground glowed in the moonlight; occasional dust devils imitated whirling dervishes on the pine-rich hills to the south.

She parked in a small area to the east of the largest brick building. When I stepped out of the car, I felt numb with the rush of cold air. I was getting tired. Bed sounded awfully good right now.

There was another guard stationed at the door, but he merely glanced at our badges and went back to his magazine.

We went up three long marble steps to a shadowy hallway. Faintly, I could hear coughing and sleep-moaning, and the professional squeak of nurses' shoes. The air smelled of floor wax and that lingering, warm, almost oppressive smell of cafeteria food.

"There's an elevator at the end of the hall," Pam said, pointing.

We went down there, me feeling like a burglar all the way, it being late and people sleeping behind the doors we passed. Troubled sleep, or they wouldn't have been here. They didn't need early waking.

The elevator was tomb-narrow and mine-car rickety.

Pam smiled. "Don't worry. It's safe," she said,

drawing my attention to the inspection sticker on the wall.

"Can I get that in writing?"

"With all the derring-do you've been involved in, Michael, I wouldn't think a shaky elevator would bother you." She frowned. "But then, Jack was always that way. No problem going into space, but let me drive a little bit over the speed limit and he got very uptight. Fast cars scared him."

I wondered if she was aware of the past tense.

I'd punched the button for the third floor without even thinking about it. The trip up was slow, and we finished the rest of it in silence.

The hallway was completely dark except for an occasional night light plugged into a wall socket every forty feet or so. To our right was a partially opened office door. Light angled out from it onto the newly polished floor. I could smell sweet pipe tobacco.

"Dr. Finebaum," I said.

"What?"

"That's his office." I pointed to the door.

"God," she said. "That's kind of scary, you know?"

I didn't answer her. "Come on. I think we should talk to him first."

She led me up to the door, peeked in.

I could see her ready herself for a quick

bright greeting. But the longer she peered into the office, the more disappointed she looked.

"Nobody's in there."

"You're sure?"

"There's just an outer office and it's empty."

"Maybe he's in the john."

"Maybe." But she didn't sound convinced.

Squeaking shoes turned me around. I faced a very tiny but very determined-looking nurse. Despite her military manner, she was the kind of fiftyish, gray-haired woman who had kept her pretty face.

"Can I help you?" she asked.

Pam spoke before I could. "We've come to see Dr. Finebaum. Is he in?"

Mentioning the doctor's name seemed to reassure the nurse. There was no nameplate on the door.

"Dr. Finebaum's missing."

"Missing?"

The nurse nodded. "For four days now."

"But what happened?"

"We don't know. He's just—gone." She shook her head, looking sad, some of the toughness gone from her now.

"No wonder he hasn't called me back the past few days."

"Yes. Is there something else I can do for you? I've got to get back to my work."

"No, thank you. We'll see ourselves out."

The nurse nodded good-bye to both of us and left.

"That's so strange," Pam said.

"Finebaum missing?"

"Uh-huh."

By now, of course, I wondered if Dr. Finebaum's absence had anything to do with Jack Campbell. Had he seen Campbell on his last day before disappearing? That seemed like a reasonable place to start.

"Watch the hall."

"What?"

"Watch the hall. I'm going to look around his office."

"Oh. Good idea."

I was tired, and I seemed to have used up my day's allotment of talent. Rather than trying to get information from the room psychically—something that's hard to do from a room, anyway; it generally works better with a single object and a specific goal—I decided to do a quick physical search to see what I could find.

It was one room with a messy desk and three equally messy filing cabinets. Looked like my own informal office in my apartment. There was a *National Geographic* calendar with a truly spectacular color photograph of a South Sea Island at dusk. There was a framed photograph of Dr. Finebaum, presumably anyway, with his attractive wife and shy little boy. There was a lot of love in that photograph and now, given the divorce, a lot of sadness. I also found a stack of magazines that ran to *Time* and *New Republic* and a stack of paperbacks that ran to Luke Short and Marcia Muller and Theodore Sturgeon. Dr. Finebaum appeared to be an eclectic sort. I sensed a kindred spirit.

I spent five minutes searching for his daily log, finally finding it under a textbook on schizophrenia.

I looked at his entries for those twenty-four hours.

Patients seen:
Gonzalez (30 min.)
Prescott (45 min)
Brice (30 min)
Group (1 hr)
Campbell (4 hrs)

Four hours? Did doctors ever spend four hours with one patient? What was going on?

I put in another five minutes looking for his keys, which he likely left in his drawer at the end of the day. I found them, surprisingly enough, right in a drawer as I'd suspected. The trouble was, the drawer happened to be in an old desk that somebody had shoved into a closet.

"God, what're you doing in there?" Pam said, peeking into the office.

"Taking a nap."

"I can believe it. Michael, we have to hurry. That nurse is liable to come back."

I needed the patient chart with the appropriate room numbers before the keys would do me much good. That link I'd had with Jack seemed to have dissolved. My shoulder had even quit hurting.

I found the chart easily. It was right beneath his log, which had been right beneath his textbook on schizophrenia.

Jack Campbell was in Room 221.

I went through the keys, found the one marked 221, and then left the office.

"C'mon," I said, taking Pam's arm, walking quickly.

"Where to?"

"Your husband's room."

"Great. I was hoping you'd say that."

I laughed softly. "You may be just as crazy as I am."

"Or even crazier."

"Yeah," I said. "I've thought of that, too. That you're even crazier."

14

There is a smell that comes to some of those who are gravely ill and dying slowly. It is a sweet smell, the ironically sweet smell of decay, and it lingers in the nose long after all other smells have vanished.

Even before I'd turned the key to Room 221, even before I'd quite opened the door, I could smell the slow, wretched death that Jack Campbell was dying.

This end of the hospital floor was in deep shadow, punctuated by faint coughs and the even fainter squeak of bedsprings. A furnace rumbled into life somewhere inside the walls, and a woman, far away, called out someone's name in her weary sleep.

Campbell's was a small room, single bed, bureau, mirror, table piled with paperbacks, a box of Whitman's chocolates with the cellophane intact, several religious items including a black rosary and a small framed painting of a sad-looking Jesus, and three boxes of snack foods, including something called Screaming Yellow Zonkers, none of them opened.

Through his barred window, you could see a ridiculously pastoral holiday scene, moonlight the color of gold sparkling on a white snowy hill where someone had built a Mr. and Mrs. couple from snow, each with cocked cute hat, each with festive red scarf and coal black buttons down the merry white belly. No hint of the place that overlooked it—all the grief and sorrow and terror, riding the lightning on the electroshock table, sitting in a shabby robe in a shabby chair while your family looked you over on sunny Sunday visits and were not necessarily reassured by what they saw.

Pam pushed past me, rushing to her husband's side. She called out to him, took his hand, touched his face, but his eyes never even blinked.

I closed the door, turned on a small reading lamp on the stand next to Campbell's bed, the darkest of the shadows scurrying away.

I went over, perched on the edge of the bed, and stared at Campbell.

He sat there in a pair of new blue pajamas and stared straight ahead at the wall.

I looked Jack Campbell over.

If I didn't know better, I would have put his age at somewhere around eighty. Oh, the thinning hair was still black, and the body was still slender, and the shoulders were still straight, but he was an old man. The flesh had begun to go, to hang like too-loose clothing, and the mouth was a thin slack line, with a froth of spittle at each end. He looked twice as old as he should, ancient compared to the man he'd been when we had done our mind-scan experiments.

Pam turned to me, and I could sense the tears she was holding back. "What's wrong with him?" she asked.

I didn't know if she expected an answer or not. I only knew I didn't have one to give her.

At least, not yet.

I closed my eyes, reaching toward that place inside me where images dwell, seeking for the calm I needed to do my work. I didn't know if I had anything left or not, but I had to try.

As I stretched out my hand toward him, my left shoulder started to throb, the pain quickly building to a sharp biting agony. I'd been reaching for his forehead, but as the pain increased I shifted my aim, seizing the material of his new blue pajamas and giving a sharp yank.

The material tore away, leaving his shoulder exposed. I heard Pam gasp, and I opened my eyes.

It was a tattoo, a small heart, with the name "Pamela" wrapped around it on a pink ribbon.

"That's new," she said. "He had a habit of al-

ways doing one crazy thing before each
mission—sort of a symbol, I guess. For his very
first mission ever, he parachuted out of a plane.
For his second, he went bungee jumping." She
gave a sad little smile. "Needless to say, his superiors were not pleased. But that was Jack."

"And this time he got a tattoo?"

She smiled again. "Yes. Okay, maybe it's not
in the same league as skydiving and bungee
jumping, but I thought it was kind of cute."

I frowned, bending down to examine the tattoo. There was no sign of infection, nothing to
indicate why that area would be causing Jack so
much pain—and that, of course, was the expla-
nation for my own pain. I was feeling what he
was feeling. I just didn't know why.

Pam grew serious, looking at her husband once
more. "What's wrong with him, Mr. Raines? Are
you getting anything?"

I started to answer her, and then I saw it and
I suppose I gave a little dramatic start, the way
people do in books and movies when they see
something astonishing.

"What's wrong?"

"I saw something. In his eye."

"Something—like a flicker—of orange? Very
deep in his eyes?"

"You saw it, too?"

"Yes, but I thought I'd just imagined it."

"But if we both saw it . . ."

I leaned forward, taking a penlight from my jacket. In my profession, or really professions plural, a penlight often comes in handy. But instead of making somebody say aaah, I generally use it on locks I'm trying to break. I'd tried psychokinesis a few times, but it never worked for me. I got a good, hard two-day headache for my trouble and nothing more.

I flashed the light into his right eye.

The first thing I noticed was that he didn't blink. No autonomic nervous system response at all.

The second thing I noticed was that the distant pulsing orange light was gone.

I examined him carefully.

I spoke his name. He didn't respond in any way.

I raised his hand and held it in mine and dragged the edge of a sharp key across his palm. No response at all.

Finally, I stepped on his bare toes. He sat there unmoved.

Some kind of trauma had put him into shock, all right.

I sighed, feeling my weariness once again. There was only one way I was going to find out anything. I thought briefly about the little vial in my pocket. This might be the night when I broke down and tried it.

I hoped I wouldn't need to.

I closed my eyes again, and tried to reach Jack. I got nothing, no sense of the man at all. I tried again, but still nothing happened.

After a moment, I opened my eyes and looked at Pam. "I sure hate to ask you this, but would you mind leaving the room?"

"I'd really like to stay."

"I'm sorry, Pam. People standing around make me self-conscious."

She looked hurt. "God, he's my own husband."

"Please, Pam."

She stared at Jack with great longing and great sorrow and then abruptly leaned toward him and kissed him on the forehead. In that instant, I saw her close her eyes and in doing so she silently told me how much she loved this man.

"I'll be down the hall."

"Thanks."

"If you need anything—"

"I appreciate it."

"You really want me to leave, don't you?"

"Uh-huh."

"God, I'm being so foolish. It's just—"

Then she was opening and closing the door, and she was gone. Reaching after the stillness once more, I placed my hand upon his brow, feeling the heat raging within him, and opened myself to his pain.

15

Back in the late sixties, several top Russian scientists conducted an experiment with a famous Ukrainian telepath, one Karl Nikolaiev by name. The scientists hooked Nikolaiev up to an assortment of machines that would register his bodily reactions as the scientists attempted to send him Morse code messages through telepathy. The notable thing about the study was the change in Nikolaiev's brain waves as he began to receive the telepathic signals. The brain waves began to vary widely. The Russian scientists were certain they had offered the first clinical evidence ever of telepathy's existence.

I didn't have an EEG handy, but I didn't need one to know I'd made contact. My shoulder caught fire, and I felt a sense of alienness wash over me.

I wanted to break contact and run. This was like nothing I'd ever experienced before, and it felt *wrong*. But I didn't. I kept my barriers down, and reached out further.

My first thought was that Jack Campbell was insane. I got a sense of persecution from him, the impression that he had somehow been invaded. And then, quite clearly, I caught the word *"aliens."* That was it. Nothing accompanied that word: no pictures, no memories, no thoughts, just the one word, and the sense of invasion—personal, direct invasion.

I didn't know what to make of it. Was Jack Campbell insane? Or—?

I pushed a little harder, reaching out for his mind, trying to make genuine contact, and that's when it happened. I felt a barrier fall, felt the beginnings of contact, but it wasn't Jack's mind I touched. It was something else. Something not human. Something . . . alien.

The contact lasted an instant, no longer. I got the impression of a vast consciousness, a sort of *uber* mind, perhaps a collective or gestalt intelligence, and then it—whatever it was—seemed to become aware of me, and the link was broken.

Jack started moving then.

He had been sitting perfectly still, but now, there in the small shadowy room, sweat beads broke out on his face, big and ugly as pimples, and his entire body began to shake.

And then he started making sounds.

Not words and certainly not sentences.

Just—sounds—high keening noises that kept getting higher and higher, like an engine whining its way to full capacity.

More images, suddenly: the link was back, and stronger than ever, but it was Jack I'd connected with—just Jack, with no sense of alienness at all. It was as though whatever had been controlling him—for that, I realized, was exactly what I'd sensed, something controlling him, or at least fighting him for control—it was as if whatever it was had pulled away from me, and in so doing had loosened its hold on Jack.

The images came in a flood, knowledge too fast and too harsh for me to assimilate all at once, but of it all, one series of images stood out. I saw a man, his face hidden from my sight, pinned naked and struggling against the bulkhead in the control room of the comet explorer. Several other astronauts were holding him while another one, the only female in the crew, disrobed. I saw her come over to him, take his face in her hands, and kiss him passionately. He must have bitten her, because her face came away bloody, but she only smiled.

And it didn't end there. I watched as she brought him into her, and at the moment of penetration I saw his face. It was Jack Campbell.

The vision ended soon after, but not before I

saw the flash of orange light deep within the woman's eyes.

Jack screamed, then, as the flood of images trickled off—the real Jack, not the one in my head.

I don't think I've ever heard anybody scream in just that way. I wanted to cover my ears. There was so much sorrow, and so much fear in his scream, that I could not endure it.

The door was thrown open and there stood the nurse and Pam Campbell.

"What the hell's been going on in here, anyway?" the nurse said. "I thought you two had left."

"I was just trying to talk to him."

"And he started screaming like this?"

I nodded.

She went over, lifted his lifeless arm, took his pulse.

Campbell had slipped back into catatonia. His eyes were closed.

His pajamas were soaked. In the past few minutes, he'd sweated so much that he'd made a mess of them.

The nurse and Pam helped him stand up—eyes still closed, mouth still slack—and got him out of the wet pajamas and into new dry ones.

The nurse pulled back the covers on the bed, plumped the pillow, and then led him over and laid him down.

She was turning back to me when I saw his eyes open and just for a moment, a faint flare of orange appear deep in his right eye.

The nurse didn't see it.

Jack Campbell closed his eyes again.

Now there was nothing to see.

"What were you doing in here, anyway? I thought you came to see Dr. Finebaum." She was angry. "This is a security facility. You can't—"

"He's my husband." Pam said it in a quiet voice, but her words stopped the nurse's voice as effectively as a shout.

"Your—? Then you're— My God, Mrs. Campbell, you shouldn't be here. It isn't safe."

"But—"

This time I was the one who interrupted. "She's right, Pam," I said. I was starting to get a handle on some of what I'd picked up from Jack. Not enough to really know what was going on, but enough to start to get some sense of it. "We have to leave."

Pam didn't move, her eyes searching mine for some sign that I knew what I was talking about. She must have found something, because after a moment she nodded.

I turned to the nurse. "Can you cover for us?"

She nodded. From what little I was able to pick up from her, I knew we could trust her. Besides, we had no choice.

"You better get going," she said. "This place is about to go nuts. The other patients will have heard Mr. Campbell, here, and they're bound to respond."

I listened. She was right. There was some kind of jungle communication going on, mind to mind, soul to soul; you could feel the tension and the anxiety—one of the animals (one Jack Campbell, to be precise) had been hurt in some way and maybe now they would be hurt.

It wasn't quite 4:30 AM yet and the patients were up and moving around, slap slap slap of slippers, deep phlegmy morning coughs, and quick rumbling voices.

The madhouse had become—a madhouse.

"Let's go, Pam."

She hesitated only a moment, watching the nurse turn back to minister to her husband, then she went over to the bedside, leaned over, and kissed her husband once on the lips. Remembering what I'd seen in his mind, I got an uncomfortable feeling about that, but I couldn't think of anything to do, so I kept quiet. She straightened after a moment, touched him lightly on the cheek, and then turned and followed me out of the room.

She didn't say a word until we were back in her car and pulling out onto the street. Around us, the night was showing signs of loosening its hold on the world, though I knew from my watch that it would hang on for another couple of hours yet.

"You peeped him, didn't you?" she asked as we headed to her car. "Jack, I mean."

"A little bit."

"And?"

"From what I could gather, there's something big going on. NASA's covering something up—which, I guess, is why Jack's here and not at some government hospital somewhere. No reporter in the world would think to look for your husband in Hastings House."

"But why? What could they possibly be covering up?"

I told her about the impressions I'd gotten, about that sense of alienness, and the other mind I'd touched. I did, however, decide to keep the images of what had occurred on board the ship to myself.

"My God," she said. "What does it all mean?"

"That's what I was wondering," I said.

We were quiet for the next several miles.

She didn't seem to have a direction, just seemed to be driving aimlessly while she thought. I was tired, though, and ready to call it a night. "I'd appreciate you giving me a ride over to a friend of mine's place."

That seemed to pull her out of her fog. "Not just yet," she said.

"Oh?"

"There's someplace we need to go first," she said, glancing over at me.

"Where?"

"The White House."

"Right," I said. "And after we finish visiting the President, maybe we can drop in on the Pope."

"The President," she said, "used to be one of Jack's best friends."

And so we went to the White House.

16

The White House affects Washingtonians the same way the Empire State Building affects New Yorkers. Natives of both cities seldom, if ever, visit their world-famous monuments. It's enough to know they're there, and enough to know what they symbolize, and enough to let the tourists make all the fuss.

As many times as I'd driven past 1600 Pennsylvania Avenue, I never really thought I'd visit it, especially when I looked at all the security precautions that were taken after the bomb scare a few years back——the phalanx of armed Marines at all entrances, the tanklike vehicles facing out spaced at intervals of one hundred yards all the way around the grounds, and the black Dobermans padding back and forth, back and forth, just the inside of the iron fence.

The city was just starting to come alive with an invasion of Metro buses with the big bug-yellow eyes in the rolling fog and morning frost, and the cars were starting their treks to the Pentagon and the Justice Department and Internal Revenue and all the other giant bureaucracies that make up D.C.

We sat two blocks down from the White House, talking. "Twenty more minutes and I'll call him." She nodded to her cellular phone mounted between us.

"Twenty more minutes, right."

"God, you still don't believe me?"

"I'm not sure."

"Why don't you read my mind and find out?"

"Because that isn't how it works."

"Reading somebody's mind?"

"Right."

"Then tell me how it works. I'm curious."

I sighed and looked out the window. The White House dominated the landscape, of course. I thought of all the sunrises and sunsets that the House had seen in the past two centuries. If you want to get a sense of history, and a sense of your own fleeting mortality, sort back through a couple hundred years of historical events. Through the icy window, against a sky turning cerulean blue, the White House looked imposing and majestic.

I picked up the large paper cup of coffee I'd bought at McDonald's half an hour ago and as I sipped the last of it, I told her.

"You need a little time, for one thing," I said.

"For what?"

"It's like trying to find your wavelength. I need to tune you in. That takes a couple of minutes."

"You just never tap right into somebody's mind?"

"Once in a while, in a very stressful situation, that happens. But it's not very common."

"So you need a few minutes."

"Right. And then you need to see how deeply you can probe."

"I guess I don't understand."

"There was a Russian named Durov back in the 1920s. His theory was that before we learned language, the human race was telepathic. And he believed that we retained some of our old defenses without quite knowing it."

"Meaning what?"

"Meaning that millions of years ago, we could not only communicate mind to mind, we could also put up blocks against other people reading our own minds."

"And we've kept that ability?"

"Apparently. And I think it happens pretty much instinctively. On a subconscious level, we understand that somebody is trying to root around in our thoughts, so we automatically set up this block. I can do it consciously."

"How about my husband? Did he put up a block?"

"Definitely. It took me a long time to pick up anything from him."

She picked up her own coffee, sipped at it. "That's what I need to convince Bob of."

"Bob?"

"Haskins. The President."

"Ah."

"None of your sarcasm. First of all, he needs to believe what you tell them. And then he needs to start an investigation into the whole comet project. I haven't told you everything yet. I thought I'd wait till we were with Bob."

"He's really going to let you in?"

"He's really going to let me in." She looked at me and smiled sadly. "He was my graduation date in college. Jack had dumped me a few months earlier. Bob used to have this incredible crush on me."

"No wonder he'll see you. Everybody's always curious about old girlfriends."

"And old boyfriends, too. There're a couple of mine I still think about from time to time."

She glanced down at the cellular phone.

"When we get in there, speak up nice and clear. Don't be intimidated."

"All right," I said.

"And tell him you voted for him."

"I didn't. I think he's kind of a showboat, in fact."

"Well, for God's sake, lie. Tell him how glad you are to meet him."

"All right."

"And be sure to compliment him on the Oval Office. His wife just redecorated it. I'll make a fuss over it and you go along."

"If you say so."

"And when you see the photo of him in his space suit, kind of ooh and aah."

"His space suit?"

"Most people forget. He was in the astronaut program for three years, but he finally had to give it up because of his ears."

"His ears?"

She tapped her right lobe. "An inner-ear infection that the medical people could never get a handle on. Causes him to be dizzy a lot."

"I see."

"But he's still an astronaut groupie. In fact, his three or four best friends are all NASA alumni. It's kind of like a good ole boys club. Anyway, when you see his photograph, make a big deal of it."

I laughed. "You'd be great at palace politics. You really know how to do all this stuff."

"You have to when you're a woman. It's one of the few weapons that men can't take away from you." She took a deep breath and stared down at the cellular phone as if it were a religious icon.

"Well," she said, touching my hand as if for luck, "here goes." She picked up her cellular phone and dialed. A few minutes later, she was talking to the President.

Then she drove up to the White House gate. A panel truck marked STERLING FLORIST suddenly pulled in ahead of us. The guard nodded to the truck and passed him inside.

When we pulled up, the guard said, "He said to apologize to you. The guy in the truck. He delivers flowers here every morning and this morning he's late."

"Well," Pam said, "I'm in the holiday spirit, so I suppose I'll forgive him." She smiled. She had a good one.

"So you're saying that something happened on the first comet exploration mission?"

"Yes, Mr. President. Exactly."

"Please, Pam. It's 'Bob.' What do you think happened?"

"I'm not sure. But—something."

"How about you, Mr. Raines? Do you have any ideas, based on your time with Jack this morning."

I shrugged. "I'm afraid not."

"But you agree with Pam that something *did* happen up there?"

"Yes."

Half an hour ago, I'd found myself being admitted through the lower-level West Wing, then walking down an impressive hall of antique grandfather clocks and expensive framed paintings of previous Presidents and then past several offices where the Cabinet members worked, according to Pam, and finally into the Oval Office itself, which was laid out more like a small apartment, with small facing couches, a fireplace with an oversized mantel, and a huge rug with the Presidential seal sewn into it. There were mementos everywhere of President Haskins' earlier years in the military, in the state legislature, and finally in the United States Senate.

I'd given the President of the United States my strongest handshake. At six-four, with a fullback's shoulders and a body that had spent four years in the Marines, President Robert Haskins had been eager to give it right back to me.

He squeezed my fingers just hard enough to make me wince. And when he smiled with that mouthful of Hollywood teeth, I knew that he was congratulating himself on being the most macho guy in the room, even though he was dressed in a blue cardigan and white shirt and gray slacks and tasseled oxblood loafers and looked goofy as hell.

But that was all forgotten, now that Pam had started telling him about Jack.

Haskins sat behind his desk, taking notes on a long yellow legal pad.

"Pam, would you tell me about your visit with Jack one more time?"

"About his condition?"

"Please."

She glanced at me, then looked back at the President while I sat there trying not to be impressed. So I was sitting in the Oval Office? No need to get excited. I was just here on business. Nothing more. Being blasé isn't always easy.

Just as Pam was about to speak again, I saw something gray-striped and furry streak through the door.

"Family cat," Haskins said. "Whiskers."

And the family cat chose just then to make her first public appearance of the day by jumping up on the President's desk and giving Pam and me some heavy scrutiny.

"What a pretty cat," Pam said. "Any special kind?"

"They're called Egyptian Maus. They're really beautiful and they've got great dispositions. We used to have a Siamese, but she wasn't what you'd call cuddly."

I reached over and petted her. She did her part by purring gratefully and holding her beautiful noble head erect.

"Anyway," Haskins said, "you were telling me about Jack, and this hospital he's in?"

She told him again, holding back nothing of what I'd told her, including about my abilities. I was afraid he was going to ask me to prove it, and even more afraid that I wouldn't be able to. Exhaustion had really caught up with me.

But he didn't ask. In fact, after the handshake thing, he barely looked at me. All his attention was focused on Pam.

"Jack's still at the hospital?" he said.

"Yes."

"What are you planning on doing?"

"I'm not sure. A lot of it depends on why he's there. I mean, if I can get better care for him elsewhere, I'm damn well going to move him. But I can't really do that until I know who ordered him there, and what's wrong with him. And that's where you come in." She leaned forward. "I mean, you and Jack were always great friends and—"

He held up his hand. "Pam, you don't have to convince me of anything. I care a lot about Jack. A lot. And I think you know that. But even if I didn't know Jack, given everything you've told me this morning, I'd sure as hell get an investigation going."

There was an air of speechifying about it all, I guess, but I suppose that's an occupational hazard, always sounding just a little gassy and political no matter what you say.

But he looked concerned, his otherwise handsome face craggy now with worry lines.

"Boy," Pam said, "could I use a bathroom."

"Always that little 'pea-size' bladder, as Jack used to call it." Haskins stood up. "C'mon. I'll walk you down the hall and show you where it is. I need to grab some papers for my next meeting, anyway."

He patted the cat on the head and said, "Why don't you entertain Mr. Raines while I'm gone?"

He winked at me and took Pam's arm and led her from the room.

Actually, the cat did entertain me.

She lay down on the rug in front of me and started rolling left to right, then right to left, then left to right, giving me a good look at her cute white furry stomach. Done with her aerobics, she got up and did a final stretching exercise, which she combined with a huge yawn.

Then she very daintily started walking around the room.

With the President temporarily gone, I allowed myself the gee-whiz feeling of thinking of some of the other people who'd been in this room—FDR in his famous smoking jacket, Harry Truman in his rimless specs, Jack Kennedy with his rocking chair, and Richard Nixon discussing the Watergate cover-up. I got a nice touristy rush of history and felt pretty special being here. I was still trying hard not to think about Denise.

Whiskers meowed.

I couldn't see her anywhere, so I stood up and started looking around.

She was standing next to a closet door, brushing it with her right front paw, sniffing and wanting in.

"I don't think I'd better open that up, Whiskers."

She looked up at me with great contempt and then meowed again and placed her right paw on the door.

"Maybe we should wait till the President comes back."

Still the contemptuous look; still the meow.

"This could lead to the firing squad, Whiskers. I hope you know that."

I opened the door for her and saw that there was a little box pushed up against the far wall. Whiskers walked in, and just as she started to sniff around at the sand I heard voices out in the hall. I wasn't doing anything wrong—all I'd done was open a door for the family cat—but I jumped like a schoolboy who's been caught going through his parents' dresser drawers. I released the closet door, allowing it to swing shut, and crossed back over to the seat I'd had earlier.

The President and Pam came in just as I was sitting back down.

"I've got a meeting now, Pam, but I'll get to work on this yet this morning. I promise. We'll figure out what's going on." He took her hand, patted it. "But you have to promise me one thing."

"What's that?"

"If I don't find anything sinister, you'll believe me."

"Of course."

"I mean, it's possible that there's a specialist at that hospital, or something. There may not be a cover-up at all."

"It's possible. But, Bob, after everything that's happened—"

He leaned forward and kissed her gently on the cheek. "Tell you what, Pam. I'll be out of town for a few days—going down to Cape Canaveral to meet an incoming mission—but then I'll be back. And I'll look into this whole thing. But right now, I've really got to run."

He turned to me, gave me another of his killer handshakes.

"Very nice to meet you, Mr. Raines. You take care of this fine lady for me, all right?"

"My pleasure."

The President of the United States looked at his watch and said, "Damn. I'm five minutes late already. I'll have one of the guards show you out."

And with that, he strode from the room.

* * *

We hadn't made it out of the building when I realized what I'd done.

"Oh, shit," I said.

"What?" Pam asked.

"I think I locked Whiskers in the closet."

"You what?"

I told her what had happened.

She laughed. "That's all right. I'll just call Bob and—"

"God, no," I said. "I don't want to look stupid in front of the President of the United States. Wait here. I'll go let the cat out, and that'll be that."

And so, five minutes later, I was back in the Oval Office, this time alone. I headed straight over to the closet, thinking about my own cat, Tasha, as I did so, and opened the door.

Whiskers was there, standing just inside the door, a sort of annoyed look on her cute little face. I chuckled softly as I watched her walk out, her tail held high.

I was just turning to leave when I felt it: that same sense of alienness I'd felt from Jack, earlier. Instinctively, I stepped into the closet, letting the door swing partly shut behind me.

A moment later, Bob Haskins walked into the room.

He didn't stay long. Just went over to his desk and got some papers. But he stayed long

enough. At one point, when he looked up at the
sound of a guard passing in the hallway, I got a
good long look at his eyes. And at the bright orange light that flashed briefly deep within
them.

The President was one of them.

I waited five minutes, until my shaking had
died down, and then followed him out. I had to
tell Pam what I'd just seen.

17

December 3

Wendy had a mother in New Jersey who always said, "You could never have been an astronaut back when I was your age, honey. They had women in the space program, but only as secretaries and file clerks and such. Not as astronauts from Trenton, New Jersey."

And in a way, her mom was right. Who ever would have thought that little Wendy Abronowitz, of the big dark eyes and the kind of sad little smile, would grow up to one day be doing a space walk a quarter of a million miles above the Earth?

But Wendy always tempered her mother's glee with a little reality. Sure, women had made some great strides, but even now— Well:

A) Colonel Jacobs was still the only woman who had ever achieved that rank.

B) Several of the male astronauts in the

program—including two of her instructors—had hit on her at various times, in ways that crossed the line of harassment and bordered on abusive.

And C) Wendy knew that she was never going to rise far above her present rank because a speech she'd given on feminist principles to some of the new recruits had greatly angered an important senator, who apparently still believed that the most natural place for a man to rest his hand was on a woman's behind. "I get goddamned sick and tired of taxpayer money going to pay some lezzie to talk about how much she hates men," the esteemed senator had said.

"Lezzie." (God, what a ridiculous-sounding word that was.)

Right.

But actually, she had to admit, there weren't all that many men she liked.

For instance, of all the men in her class, there was only one she really trusted, the moody, quiet Dwight Malone. Maybe because Malone had lost his first wife to breast cancer, he seemed to be a lot more sensitive to women. No strutting macho bullshit. No sly come-ons. She liked him enough that she'd even had an idle daydream or two about going to bed with him. If the good senator only knew how much Wendy enjoyed good old heterosex—the birth control implant in her upper left arm should prove that—he might quit calling her a lesbian.

Wendy thought of Malone now, and how much she missed him. He'd been one of the three Americans assigned to the first comet mission, and she'd been unable to find out anything about him since it left. Weird. And more than a little scary.

Wendy tried to pull her attention back to the task at hand. Free-walking in space, tied to a moving ship by nothing more than a thin tether, was not the time for idle woolgathering. Still, there was just something about the vastness of space that seemed to invite quiet thinking. It didn't matter if it was a summer evening back in Trenton, sitting on the back porch and staring up at the twinkling stars above, or a walk in the dark around the space station *Freedom,* the stars just seemed to invite philosophy and introspection.

They lay all around her, fireflies in the night sky, and she shook her head at her own inability to express the wonder she saw. She'd read all the books the early astronauts had written about their first space walks. She'd seen the first color pictures sent back from the moon, showing the Earth as a startlingly blue ball hanging in the night. Of them all, she thought that maybe Frank Borman had said it best, but not even he had come anywhere close to capturing the reality of swimming with the stars.

She smiled, enjoying the sight of the ship motionless against the backdrop of stars. In reality, the ship was moving quite fast, but there was no hint of that from where she was. Only the controls on board showed that they were even moving.

"Hey, Abronowitz," Miriam Goldmann said in Wendy's ear. "You're moving kind of slowly. You find something wrong or you lost in space again?"

Wendy chuckled. "God, Miriam, sometimes I can't believe we're really doing this, you know? I mean, talk about a dream come true."

"I know, Wendy. Sometimes—" She broke off.

"Miriam? What is it?"

Goldmann was silent for a moment. Then she said, "Ah, nothing. I've just got a creepy feeling. I swear, everyone on board is watching me. It's like they're taking turns, first Varnov, then Jacobs, then Nablokov, then Martinelle, then Varnov again. Like clockwork. Every time I glance up, one of them's looking at me."

"Miriam—"

Goldmann sighed. "I know, Abronowitz. Paranoia and depression are normal symptoms of long space missions. Still . . ." She sighed. "It's just creepy, that's all."

Wendy chuckled again and went back to work.

Jacobs had sent her out to check the heat shielding. It was a ridiculous task. After all, re-entry wasn't for nearly three weeks yet, but when the commander said, "Do this," you did it, and did it well.

She went in a spiral path, crossing and re-crossing the surface of the craft, looking for any tiles that might have come loose during the flight. Her movements were automatic, the slow-motion ballet that she'd worked so hard to learn. In her ears, she could hear the hissing of her own breathing and, beneath that, the muted hum of the radio link keeping her in touch with the craft.

She'd been out of the ship for thirty-three minutes when Goldmann spoke again.

"Hey, Abronowitz," she said, her voice barely above a whisper.

"I'm here."

"God, it's really getting creepy in here. I caught Varnov watching me a minute ago, and I could have sworn I saw that orange light in his eyes. I don't know—"

There was a sudden commotion on the line, a burst of noise that might have been anything. Wendy heard Miriam draw in her breath sharply, followed by what might have been a muffled cry, and then, as abruptly as the slamming of a door, her comm line went dead.

Years of training kicked in, fighting back the panic that was her first reaction. Automatically, she checked to make sure that her tether was still connected to the ship. When she saw that it was, she returned to her task.

Whatever the problem was, there were people in the ship who would take care of it. That's one of the lessons you learned in the program: no one could do it all. You had to be able to trust your crewmates with your life, or no mission could ever succeed.

Slowly she went back to checking the tiles, but now she no longer noticed the stars. That muffled cry still echoed in her ears, and she couldn't help worrying about what was happening. Maybe they were right; maybe this mission really was jinxed.

TWO

TWO

18

"Are you sure?"

"I'm sure."

"It was an orange light just like Jack's?"

"Just like Jack's."

"And you didn't try to peep him?"

We were driving through the streets of Washington. Pam's knuckles were white on the wheel.

I sighed. "No, I didn't, Pam. For one thing, I've done more peeping in the last twenty-four hours than I have in I don't know how long, and I'm tired. Besides, if this thing, whatever it is, really *is* a collective mind, then it's got some form of telepathy of its own. The last thing I wanted was for him to sense me there, to realize that I was on to him."

She thought it over. I had to admire the way she accepted it and moved forward. "Then we can't trust him, can we? Bob, I mean?"

"I don't think so."

"He's the President of the United States, and we can't trust him."

"Where're you going?"

"The hospital. I want to get Jack."

"And take him where?"

"Anywhere. I'm worried about him, now that Bob knows we've found him."

"That's a good idea."

"I'm glad you approve." Beat. "Sorry. I get bitchy sometimes when I'm scared."

"We all do."

"He's the President of the United States, and we can't trust him. I just can't get over that."

"Here's the turn."

"I have to tell you backseat drivers really piss me off?"

"I'm in the front seat."

"You know what I mean."

"I just thought you might not see it, being that you're a little preoccupied right now."

"Just because I'm a little preoccupied right now doesn't mean that I'm not driving well. You're forgetting that my father was—"

"—a test driver."

"Are you making fun of him?"

"Why don't I just shut up and let you drive."

"That's a very good idea. Especially the part about you just shutting up."

There wasn't much I could say to that.

The hospital looked a little less prisonlike in the early morning light. For one thing, obstinate red rider-plows worked over the sidewalks, spewing geysers of snow behind them, all hard hearty holiday work that would be rewarded with turkeys and cranberries and pumpkin pie with whipped cream, and holiday stockings packed with goodies of every kind, for people of every kind. For another, a few of the patients were all bundled up and building snowmen on the lawn of the administration building. They were merry and industrious, and when they laughed it was the pure silver laughter of children.

The gates were open now, it being regular visiting hours, though there was still a guard in the little shack. Pam gave him a wave as she pulled in, then drove on through. She found a parking space, and we got out and started walking up to the front of the administration building.

"Sorry I was so shitty back there."

"We're tired," I said. "Both of us. No big deal."

"Are you hungry? I'm starving."

"We'll get Jack someplace safe and then we'll go have this huge breakfast."

"God, that sounds good," Pam said, eyes starting to tear, nose starting to redden in the cold.

The administration building smelled of furnace heat and rubber runners damp from snow-covered boots.

We found a pebbled glass door with ADMIN-ISTRATOR printed in black, and went in.

A gray-haired woman with a pince-nez and a matching blue sweater outfit sat working over an old Royal electric with terrifying competence. Two fingers and she must have been doing ninety, a hundred words a minute.

She stopped and looked up. "May I help you?"

Pam said, "I'd like to see the administrator, please."

"Who may I say is calling?"

"Mrs. Campbell. Mrs. Jack Campbell. My husband's in room 221."

"Oh. Of course. Why don't you have a seat right over there?"

"Thank you."

"And may I help you, sir?"

"I'm with her. With Mrs. Campbell."

Her look said that she did not approve of the fact that I was with Pam.

"I see," she said.

We went over and sat down. The secretary pressed an intercom button and asked if Mr. Frazier could see us now and he said, "Yes," in a woofy sort of way through a cheap tinny speaker; and then the inner office door opened up and a man who resembled the old-style Russian premier on the order of Khruschev, I suppose, came striding out to greet us with a magnificently insincere smile and the wettest hand I've ever shaken.

When Pam said that what she had to say was private, he said, "Of course," and led us into his office, then stood aside while we got comfortably seated in his leather guest chairs. He closed the door then came round and sat on the other side of the desk and said, "Now, Mrs. Campbell, how may I help you?"

"I want to get my husband."

"'Get' him?"

"Pack up his clothes and take him."

"But that's impossible."

"I'm his wife. I'm assuming he's not under any court order to be institutionalized or anything like that."

But Frazier shook his square gray bureaucratic head. "I'm surprised you don't know."

"Know what?"

He sat back plumply in his plump chair, in his plush tan office with the fresh cut flowers in a tan vase on his tan desk, and said, "I don't know why they wouldn't have contacted you. That's standard procedure."

"Who're you talking about, Mr. Frazier?"

He sat forward on his elbows. "The head of our board of trustees. He phoned here about twenty minutes ago and said that I wasn't to let anyone see Mr. Campbell under any circumstances. Now, I have to admit, I didn't specifically ask him about you—you must realize, I did not know Mr. Campbell even had a wife—but still, his instructions were clear. No one is to see the patient for any reason."

The sun was out and sparkling brilliantly off the white hills filling Frazier's west windows. Everything looked clean and new. In contrast to here—where the long grappling arm of the federal government had seized Pam by the throat.

"I'm his wife. You can't keep me from seeing him, and you can't keep him here without a court order."

"On the contrary, Mrs. Campbell," he said. "You did not admit him to this hospital. You have not even shown me any evidence that you actually are his wife. If you are, and if you have grounds for moving him, then I suggest you get a court order, because without one you will not be allowed to see him. Those are my orders."

"Orders!" Pam said.

She started to say something more, but I flashed on our good Mr. Frazier and held up my hand.

"It's no use, Pam," I said. "His mind's made up. Let's just go."

"But—"

Mr. Frazier stood up. "Wait, Mrs. Campbell. Perhaps we should discuss—"

"Pam," I put a slight edge to my voice, and tried to signal her with my eyes, "let's *go*."

She seemed to catch my meaning, or at least my urgency, because she gave a little nod and stood up. She did pause long enough to deliver one more shot to the administrator, however.

"You have not heard the last of this," she said, and then we left.

Outside the office, even before we'd made it back to the reception area, she turned to me. "All right, Michael. What's up?"

Somewhere during the course of our evening together, I'd gone from Mr. Raines to Michael.

"I was too tired to do a full read of Mr. Frazier, but I did catch something. He actually did get that call from the head trustee, and he did receive those orders."

"But—"

"But that's not all, Pam. He also learned that several government agents would be showing up soon to question anyone who asked for Jack Campbell. He was just trying to stall us until they arrived."

"Government agents? But—"

"Yes. I'd say your old friend Bob is a fast mover."

We had just cleared the vestibule and were stepping outside when I saw a gunmetal gray Ford pulling up in the lot six or seven spaces from Pam's car.

I grabbed her, pulled her back inside, up the stairs.

"What's going on?" she said, her heels clicking on the wooden floor.

"Our friends are here. We'll wait till they get up to Frazier's office, then we'll sneak out."

"I'm scared," she said.

I wanted to say that I was, too, but maybe she'd mistake me for the hero-type if I didn't.

19

We walked briskly down the steps, briskly down the walk, briskly to her car.

We got in, yanked on the seat belts. Just as she was firing up the engine and stepping on the gas, I happened to raise my eyes and look up at Frazier's window. One of the agents was watching us pull out. He disappeared quickly, no doubt zooming out of Frazier's office for a quick flight outdoors.

"We've been spotted," I said.

"Hold on."

She went back to being the son her father never had, whipping the rear end around so fast we nearly skidded into an oncoming car, then straightening out and aiming the long hood toward the exit as if we were about to be catapulted.

By this time, both government men were taking the front steps two at a time.

She laid down a strip of rubber that would

have impressed any seventeen-year-old boy in the world.

Then we were flying out of the parking lot, forcing nurses in crisp white uniforms and heavy winter coats, nurses on their way to the morning shift, to jump aside and scowl at us and form silent dirty words with their lipstick red mouths.

"Any idea where we're going?" I said as she squealed us up the hill to the STOP sign that led to the street.

"My house."

"Bad idea."

"Why?"

"They'll be there already."

"The feds?"

"You bet."

"Your place?"

"Same problem."

"Then where?"

We entered the street going sixty-three. By the time we'd passed three cars, we were already up to eighty.

"You know where Dr. Finebaum lives?"

"No."

"Find a phone booth. I'll look him up."

"What're they going to do to Jack?"

I wanted to lie, tell her he'd be fine, but obviously he wasn't fine, and it was unlikely he was every going to be fine again.

"All we can do is hope for the best."

"In other words, you think they might kill him."

"Not kill him, no, but use him in some way."

"God," she said, sounding on the edge of tears, "he looked like he's suffered so much."

"I'm sorry, Pam. I truly am."

"He's such a good man. I haven't been much of a wife to him, I'm afraid."

There was a convenience store a block ahead, on the left.

She pulled in there. I got out of the car and went into the booth. I was surprised to find most of the phone book intact; B through W was anyway. The rest of the booth was typical, the glass cracked, the floor reeking of piss and vomit, and graffiti covering half the available space. It was cold enough, not much over five above, that my knuckles got numb just from this brief exposure.

There were seven Finebaums. Dr. Robert Finebaum was the fourth.

I did what all the other street punks around the world do when they want a certain address. I tore the entire sheet from the phone book.

Before going back to the car, I went into the convenience store and bought two large coffees. My knuckles were no longer frozen. They were scalding from hot coffee leaking from the flimsy paper cups.

We sat drinking our coffee, trying to figure out the fastest way to get to Dr. Finebaum's house. He lived over by Georgetown University.

"You think they'll be watching his house?"

"Of course," I said.

"Then what're we going to do?"

"Talk to his neighbors. See if they can help us."

"Won't the watchers think it's funny when we walk up to the neighbor's house?"

"No. They'll think we're there to see the neighbors."

She stared at me a long moment. "You like this sort of thing, don't you?"

"What sort of thing?"

"Cloak and dagger."

I shrugged. "I suppose."

"You're like Jack. An overgrown kid."

I smiled. "I suppose that's fair."

"Don't you worry about getting killed?"

"Sometimes."

"But not often."

I turned in the seat so I could get a better look at her. "Whatever's going on here is important. Very important. I can't just walk away from it."

She sipped coffee. "These are terrible cups. I keep waiting for them to just disintegrate."

"Tell me about it."

"May I ask you a question?"

"Sure."

"Have you scanned my mind? Since that first time, I mean."

"No."

"Really?"

"Really."

"How come?"

I laughed. "Vanity."

"Oh?"

I nodded. "A couple of years ago, I decided to tap into the mind of this woman I was dating. It was a pretty humbling experience."

"She didn't like you?"

"Let's see. She thought I was dull, she thought I was ugly, and she thought I was arrogant. And she planned to be home early so she could spend the night in bed with this bureaucrat she'd met the day before."

"So that made you gun-shy?"

"Very. The only scanning I do now is for a reason, not curiosity. And anyway, setting up an informal kind of scan isn't all that easy."

I caught her blue eyes dancing nervously in the rearview.

"They're going to find us."

"Not necessarily," I said.

"What'll happen if they do?"

"I'm not sure."

Her eyes strayed from the rearview and settled on mine. "Do you think Jack's become some sort of alien?"

"I think it's a possibility."

"And Bob—the President, I mean?"

"I think that's a possibility, too."

"God."

"I know."

"Who'd believe us if we tried to tell them?" She laughed. "We'd probably end up on one of those talk shows where people babble about being abducted by aliens."

"Except we'd be telling the truth."

"But," she said, laughing, "we'd sound just as crazy as the other people, wouldn't we?"

"Yeah, now that you mention it, we would."

She opened her door, turned her disintegrating coffee cup upside down, spilled out all the coffee, and then pitched the empty cup into a sack in the back seat.

"Have you thought that maybe Dr. Finebaum didn't run away at all—that maybe the government kidnapped him?"

"I've thought about it," I said. "But I still want to go and talk to his neighbors."

"So do I," she said, and then went back into her Indy 500 mode.

20

They were there, all right, two of them in top-coats, suits, and short haircuts sitting inside a plain blue Plymouth sedan that was pushing little gray putt-putts of smog out of its tailpipe.

The address was on 30th Street in Georgetown, an entire block of row houses, the ones the tourists love to oooh and aaah over.

"FBI?"

"Uh-huh," I said. "I gave them a quick scan."

"Get anything?"

"Just that they were sent here by your friend the President."

We were parked at the opposite end of the block. By now, 9:00 AM, most of the morning rush traffic was gone, so the feds were pretty easy to spot.

"They'll see us," she said.

"Not if we go the back way."

"Are you serious?"

"Sure. Just drive around the block and we'll park and walk back."

"Why're they there, anyway? Dr. Finebaum's gone."

"But being detectives, they think that somebody'll try and get into his row house. And then they figure they'll be able to ask some questions that may bring them a little closer to the doctor. And we're doing the same thing, by the way, hoping that somebody who knows him can tell us something useful about him."

"It's cold out there. I wish I hadn't thrown my coffee away."

"Finish mine."

A few minutes later, she made a U-turn and we drove up the block away from the blue Plymouth. It was a golden winter morning and everything looked beautiful, especially all the holiday decorations.

We went around the block, stopped, got out, and started walking.

The snow was noisy beneath our feet, squeaking and crunching, and the air felt pure and invigorating in my nostrils and lungs.

It was a pretty nice looking alley, as alleys go, all the garbage cans and dumpsters lined up neatly, the garages newly painted, and even the occasional dog turd presentable if not exactly winning.

I found the back of Dr. Finebaum's row

house, walked to the back of the house east of it, opened up a judas gate, stood back for Pam to go in, and then followed her.

Somebody warm-blooded lived here. The kitchen window was open a few inches, leaving room between window and sill for a blueberry pie to cool. I felt like a moon-eyed hungry kid. I think Pam felt that way, too. She closed her eyes and took deep breaths. "Oh, boy," she said, "it'd be so nice to be ten again and not know anything about the world. I really miss my innocence. God, I really do."

I knocked on the back door.

After a few seconds, I heard an older woman's voice saying, "We've got guests, Esmerelda. Look."

A gray cat poked her head out between lace curtains and looked us over, not seeming terribly impressed.

The little old lady who opened the door wore all the right little old lady accoutrements, from sensible black oxfords to a sensible plain apron, from sensible rimless glasses to a sensible little knit thing to hold her sensible gray bun. She had merry brown eyes.

"Are you from a church?"

"Church?" I said.

"You know, for charity."

"Oh. No. We're here because our friend is missing."

She made a wan face. "Dr. Finebaum."

"Yes. You know him?"

"Very well. We used to play Parcheesi three times a week." She smiled. "He always said he liked to live in the fast lane."

"Any idea where we can find him?"

She shook her head. "I wish I did. I'm so darned worried about him, worried that something terrible might have happened to him. You know how the world is today."

"Your pie smells great," Pam said.

"Would you like to come in and have a piece? I'd be happy to cut one for you."

"I'm afraid not," I said. "We're in kind of a hurry."

She looked at Pam and then at me. "You're not police, are you?"

"No. But we need to find Dr. Finebaum."

"Why?"

"We need to talk to him. Business."

It was an old-fashioned kitchen, not a microwave in sight, a big white gas range standing next to a big white Frigidaire that looked more like an icon than an appliance, and a little breakfast nook with a red plastic napkin holder and good china cups that were just now starting to yellow from their decades of service. The old woman had probably sat in this kitchen, or one very like it, and heard the radio bulletin about

Pearl Harbor or V-J Day, or she'd sat here and laughed with and doted on her son home from college. It was a sunny room that smelled sweet and warm with baking, a room filled with very happy ghosts.

Being the proper grandma-sort she was, she coerced us into two pieces of blueberry pie each, the second with a chunk of cheddar on the side, which was damned good actually.

"I lost my own husband six years ago," she said as she poured me my third cup of coffee. "Brain tumor. The poor man. A lot of pain, but at least he went quickly."

She sat down at the table across from us and started working on her own piece of pie and cheddar. "That's how Jason—Dr. Finebaum— and I became friends. After his wife died, he started walking alone every night. And we'd run into each other up the street in the park. So we became friends. Confidantes, I suppose you'd say, kind of supporting each other through our mourning period."

"Did he seem troubled lately?" I said.

"Tell me something."

"All right."

"Do you want to help Dr. Finebaum or hurt him? And look me in the eye when you answer. I've got a knack for telling who's being honest."

"We're on the same side," I said.

She kept staring for a while. Then she said,

"Good. You're telling the truth. Now, what was your question?"

"Did he seem troubled lately?"

She nodded, her mouth full. "About six weeks ago, I noticed that he'd stopped walking at night. Then I found out that he'd started sleeping in his office. That's what Angela told me, anyway?"

"Angela?"

"You don't know about her?"

"No," I said. "I guess I don't."

She looked at me with her grandmotherly eyes and said, "She's a thirty-year-old black prostitute." She smiled sweetly. "There. I hope you're properly shocked."

"Dr. Finebaum saw a prostitute?"

"Oh, not 'saw' her in the way you mean. Oh, once or twice, back there in the beginning, maybe he 'saw' her that way, but she became like his girlfriend. It was real sweet, real nice."

"You didn't get jealous?"

"Not at all. Jason and I discussed having a few dates one time, but then we both realized that we should be satisfied with what we had—a good strong friendship. Angela got him to come alive again. He became a much younger man when he was around her. I was very happy for him."

"Where's Angela now?"

She looked at me for a very long time, and

then she glanced briefly at Pam, and said, "You've got a little blueberry on your chin, dear."

"Oh," Pam said, dabbing at it with her white napkin from the red plastic napkin holder. "Thank you."

"They're after you, aren't they?"

"Who is?"

"The same people that are after Jason."

"And that would be—"

"—the FBI. They've been here several times. They know I'm withholding information, but they don't know what to do about it."

"What kind of information?"

"About Angela."

"What about her?"

"Where she's hiding. They knew about her, but they couldn't find her."

"You know where she's hiding?"

She looked at Pam and smiled. "He looks like he could use a tranquilizer, doesn't he?"

"It's very important," Pam said, sounding as if she could use a little tranquilizing herself. "Very important."

The woman smiled and said, "Well, you two kids don't think I'd have brought it up if I wasn't going to tell you, do you? And you know why I'm going to help you? Because I'm one of the last of the liberals. FDR, JFK, LBJ—I even liked Bill Clinton. All of which means I don't trust the FBI. If they're after Jason, then I want to help him any way I can. You understand?"

She got a pad and a pencil and wrote out an address.

"Now," she said, "how about one more piece of pie?"

Pam smiled at me, and shrugged.

How could we say no?

21

From the row house we drove over to the University. I wanted to see how many full-time people they'd assigned to hunt for us. The tan Ford with the two young men who looked like accountants gave me my answer.

"They're everywhere."

"Like Chicken Man," I said.

"Who?"

"Just showing my age. It's an old radio show."

"Now we go see Angela?" she said.

"Now we go see Angela."

I stared at the tan Ford until it faded from sight in the rearview mirror. They really were everywhere.

I felt a sudden nostalgia for the University. So much of my life was tied up in it. And now it would never be the same again.

Finding Angela's apartment house was a real job. Took two hours and we ended up in some piney hills north of Dulles Airport.

The place was twelve small units, six up six down, with some pretty vile graffiti spraypainted in black on the white paint covering the wooden walls. There were four cars in the parking lot, all of the rusted-out variety. The newest one was maybe ten years old.

Pam pulled in and we got out, walked up the stairs to Apartment 6-B. The dumpster we passed smelled sweet with rotted garbage. For a moment, I had to hold my breath.

The handrail on the open second floor hall was as rusted as the cars below. I put my hand on it and that was when the image came.

I saw: shadowy interior/apartment that had been frantically and messily searched/young attractive black woman lying on her back on the floor, perhaps dead/chunky white man in her bedroom listening to our footsteps as we approached the door.

I put a hand out and stopped Pam.

"Go down and sit in the car."

"What's wrong?"

"Please. Just do what I say."

She looked scared and frustrated and even a little hurt.

"Please," I said.

"Will you be all right?"

I nodded.

She left, a child who had been spurned by someone she trusted, shoulders slumping, moving slowly, as if in great pain.

I stood in the bright snowy morning looking at the scabrous red paint on Angela's door. Behind the door—

I saw: shadowy man in shadowy apartment/ big silver Magnum in hand/moving carefully through the living room.

Probably he would get behind the door and surprise me.

I lifted my right foot and smashed the heel down just above the wobbly gold doorknob.

The door burst inward.

Surprise had shaken him. He was raising his Magnum to fire at me—beefy man in green worsted suit, too much grease on his dark hair—but he was scared and startled, so I didn't have any problem slapping the Magnum from his hand and putting the business end of my Walther to his forehead. Incongruously, somebody had left the TV on, volume all the way down. Shemp was just now hitting Mo on the head with a hammer.

"Hey, man, you're not going to kill me or anything, are you?"

"Who are you?"

"I've got a wife and two little kids."

"You're breaking my heart. Now who are you?"

I was starting to pick up some scanning data. Couple of minutes, I'd be getting a good read and then he wouldn't have to tell me anything. All I'd have to do would be to punch it up on my mental computer.

But his dialog about the little woman and the dear sweet kiddies had relaxed me more than it should have.

He brought up a concrete knee that connected with the most sensitive area of my entire body, and then all the data I'd been scanning fled the screen and all that was left was huge red and starry black explosions of pain. He was even smart enough to pitch to the left so I couldn't find him for a good shot.

He didn't have much trouble pushing me over backward—across an ottoman—or snatching up his Magnum. He fired off two quick shots at me. I groaned, making him think I'd been hit. He didn't take the time to check. He ran out the door.

I spent a long time on the floor, groaning. I got a good look at the rough indoor-outdoor style carpet and I got an even better look at a wooden sofa leg that was so scratched and scarred, it looked as if somebody had been using a whittling knife on it.

I was just pushing up from the floor, pain still clenching my teeth and tearing up my eyes, when I saw the beefy man in the door again.

He had his hands up in the air.

Right behind him was Pam. She was smiling. She obviously couldn't help herself. "He ran past me in the parking lot, so I tripped him and got him. Pretty good, huh?"

"Pretty *damn* good," I said, then began the tortured process of getting to my feet without screaming.

22

I got him roped tight to a chair and then I hit him in the mouth a lot harder than was strictly necessary. I wanted him to be afraid of me.

"You bastard," he said, tasting blood at the corner of his mouth.

This time, more civilized, I slapped him rather than hit him.

"Bastard," he said.

From the bedroom, I heard Angela's first conscious moans. We had carried her into the bedroom, where Pam had immediately started dabbing at the nasty cut my friend had given her.

"You enjoy beating up women?"

"Up yours."

I held his wallet up again. Read off the ID. "Karl David Fenton. Domestic Intelligence. That's out of the White House?"

He just glowered at me.

I kicked him hard in the kneecap.

You could probably hear him swearing and crying a block away. I'd broken something.

"Karl, you don't seem to be getting the message. I'm going to keep working you over till you tell me what your assignment is."

The glare again.

In his way, I suppose, he was brave and dutiful. Too bad brave and dutiful wasn't what I was looking for.

I brought my heel down on his toes.

He hadn't finished crying yet from his kneecap. Probably he wouldn't finish crying for a long time. The toe-stomp seemed to addle him, as if his brain were being overloaded with pain impulses.

I gave his broken kneecap another love tap.

But he didn't talk. Just hung his head and made mewling noises.

I tried not to feel sorry for him. I'm not usually a sadist, but these were extreme circumstances and sadism was the only friend I had.

"You've got balls, Karl. I'll say that for you."

He raised his head and looked at me, and I saw then, given the stubborn hatred in his eyes, that this approach wasn't going to work at all. At least not for another six or seven hours. Ole Karl here could take more than his share of pain.

I doubled my fist and caught him just above the right temple.

His head flopped forward, his entire body straining against his ropes.

Pretty much the way I wanted him.

I've only been sexually impotent once in my life. This was a few months after my wife left me, when the emotional pain was still almost crippling, and on a night when my drinking far exceeded my usual tolerance.

I was all fumbling apologies and little embarrassed jokes and she was all calm reassurance and tender pity.

A kind of panic set in. I worried that maybe this was inexplicably a permanent condition of some sort. I lay there in the darkness, holding her, feeling ashamed and denatured.

Which was pretty much the way I felt this morning when I experienced esper impotence.

I had spent nearly an hour with my tied-up friend and as yet I hadn't raised as much as random static in my attempts to tune him in.

Pam had come out of the bedroom twice to see how I was doing. She'd hurriedly returned to the bedroom, where she had Angela sitting up and sipping hot tea. Pam must have sensed my considerable frustration.

I got up and walked outside to the open hall. It was one of those moments when I really wanted a cigarette. Some real killer carcinogens, an unfiltered Lucky Strike maybe, or a Camel.

The sun was gone, leaving a drab gray day. The rusted-out hulks of cars and the battered shape of the apartment house itself didn't do much to make things any prettier. There are certain moments when poverty takes you by the collar and shakes you till you get the point. This was one of them.

She slid her arm around my waist and leaned against me, and in that moment I liked her to an almost ridiculous degree.

"Just relax. Things'll be fine."

Pretty much what that woman had told me in bed the night I couldn't get an erection.

I grinned and pulled her to me. We probably both needed a little tenderness at the moment. "You should have been a shrink. You've got a calming effect on people."

She laughed. "Yeah—I put them right to sleep."

We gave each other a squeeze that was more brother and sister than lovers, though buried in there somewhere was an inkling of sexual desire.

"I'd better get back to Angela," Pam said. "By the way, a friend of mine asked me to check on her condo while she's gone for the holidays. We can hide Angela there. She'll be safe."

"You're a nice woman, you know that?"

"You're pretty nice yourself."

She suddenly looked uncomfortable, and her arm withdrew from my waist, and then she was walking back into the apartment.

I gave my friend in the ropes another try. Actually, I gave him three more tries, each one a little more promising than the previous one.

On the second try, I got a little static. On the third try, I started picking up random thoughts and images.

On the fourth try, I started getting hard information.

I spent twenty minutes scanning and probing. In the middle of it all, Pam came out. Her grin told me she knew that I'd finally had some luck.

By the time I finished with him, he was starting to come awake. He'd wet himself. He looked very embarrassed.

"What the hell'd you do to me, anyway?"

"Nothing much."

"I'm not going to tell you a damned thing."

He glowered at me.

He was a little crude as federal boys went. These days most of them are college grads and are pretty good on computers and probably let themselves get dragged to the ballet by their wives. Fenton was a throwback. If nothing else, his broken nose and badly damaged knuckles told you that. Goons never seemed to go all the way out of fashion. Somebody always has a use for one of them somewhere.

I untied him.

When he tried to stand up, he was shaky and had to hold on to the wobbly table.

He kept glancing down at the dark stain on his crotch and wincing.

As a bona fide goon, he was not without pride, and what bona fide goon would want it known that he had peed his pants?

He knew something was wrong—people in his line of work didn't usually just walk out of situations like these—but he couldn't quite figure out what.

"Now what?" he asked.

"You killed a lady I cared about."

"Oh, yeah?"

"Yeah. She never stood a chance, and you tortured her before killing her. And for no better reason than your own pleasure."

By now, he'd figured out what I was going to do. I raised the gun. I pulled the trigger. Part of his head tore away, like a toupee in a strong head wind.

23

December 3

Wendy stood in the air lock, waiting for it to finish its cycle. She was itching to get her helmet off again, and to find out what had happened.

When the green light came on, she quickly shut off her oxy flow and then unsealed her suit. God, it would feel good to get home and be able to shower again.

The inner lock opened and she pulled herself through. And then she stopped. There was a smell in the air, a faint, musky odor that hadn't been there before. She might not have noticed it if she hadn't been in her suit for so long, but there was something familiar about it.

She took off her suit and brought it down to the storage area. As much as she wanted to rush to the control room, the routine of shipboard life could not be broken. Her suit was top priority. Everything else had to wait. She took care of it, cleaning out the filters and recharging the tanks, and was just about to head up to the control room when she noticed it.

There was a rag jammed into the corner, near the bank of lockers. Rags were not common in space. They had a tendency to float around and get into all sorts of places where they didn't belong, but that wasn't what made this rag so unusual. No, the thing that caught Wendy's eye was the bright spot of fresh red blood on it.

The feeling of uneasiness that had been with her for some time swelled into something darker and stronger. Wendy was afraid. This ship, this mission, had been a comfortable part of her life, but now they were twisting on her, turning into something alien and terrifying. It was a feeling she hadn't had in a long time.

When she was a kid, Wendy used to play hide-and-seek with her older brother. Their big old rambling house was perfect for two kids to hide in. It went three stories, if you counted the attic, and had an unfinished basement and a root cellar. Perfect.

But there were times when she'd be hiding from Joe, and the old familiar house would take on eerie dimensions. There were the sounds of the furnace ticking away, even in the summer, its pilot light making the metal expand and contract noisily. There were the sounds of the house settling, its ancient wooden beams creaking and popping. And there were the sounds of the trees outside, the massive oaks and stately elms, their branches scrabbling against the siding and groaning in the wind.

But most of all there was the feeling of fear, of what was normally friendly and comforting suddenly becoming strange and frightening.

When she was eight, Wendy had hidden under their father's workbench. It was a dark and dusty place, with the smell of sawdust and of grease everywhere. She'd worked her way deep under the bench, squirming past shadowy piles of wood and broken tools.

It was a good place, and she thought maybe Joe wouldn't find her there, but as she worked her way backward her foot got caught in the stack of lumber her father was saving.

She tugged at it, but it wouldn't move, and the wood was too heavy for her to shift.

For a while, Wendy just lay there, listening to the sounds of the house, hoping to hear the sounds of her brother calling, "Ollie-ollie-oxen, all in free!" But the sound never came. Instead, after about twenty minutes, during which time she'd gone from hoping that Joe wouldn't find her to dreading it, she heard the most frightening sound of all: the front door slamming shut.

Joe had given up, but rather than calling for her he'd stormed out, probably in a pout. And now here she was, her ankle starting to hurt, needing to go to the bathroom, and simply wanting *out*, and there was nothing she could do.

That was the feeling Wendy had now, standing in the storage room. A radio blackout, a musky smell, and a bloody rag. Something had happened here while she was gone, something bad. It was just like that old house of theirs, the old and familiar becoming the new and strange. But this time there was a difference. This time she wasn't eight years old and helpless.

Stuffing the rag into her locker so it wouldn't float away, she turned and headed up to the control room.

It was time to get some answers.

24

Pam's friend lived in a converted Victorian near the Botanical Garden on Maryland Avenue.

It was nearly three on a grim gray day when I pulled into the rear parking lot. Fatigue was starting to take its toll on my stamina and my mood. A couple of times on the way over I'd snapped at Pam who—apparently suffering the same sort of fatigue I was—snapped right back.

Angela, an attractive thirtyish black woman who had fixed herself up in a flattering mauve knit dress and matching silk head scarf, sat in the back and smiled. "Boy, you two are really getting tired. Better ease off before you get into a fistfight."

To which Pam had said, "He doesn't look that tough."

I couldn't help it. I laughed. Scary as all this was, it also had an element of the ridiculous about it. If you couldn't trust the President of the United States, whom could you trust?

Through a back door with enough locks to keep an entire street gang at bay—up steps so steep the U.S. Olympic mountain climbing team could train here—into an apartment so elegant and pricey I was afraid to move.

Everything was white or chrome and glass except for the abstract paintings, which were done in furious reds and grim, grabbing blacks. I could almost hear the brittle patter that filled this room whenever a cocktail party was being staged.

"Angela, why don't you go get settled in. I'll see what's in the fridge."

Angela obliged. I suspected she wanted to get away from us. We were turning cranky again.

I followed Pam into the kitchen where she opened the refrigerator and started setting things out on the counter.

"BLTs," she said.

"I'm a vegetarian."

She looked at me funny. "God, no kidding?"

"Yeah. Sorry to disappoint you."

"There you go again."

"There I go again?"

"Yeah, that pissy tone of voice you get."

"Me pissy? How about you?"

"You know something—I didn't know men could have periods till I met you."

She kicked the fridge door shut with her heel and then went over to the counter.

"You going to take off your coat before you start making sandwiches?" I said.

"I'll take off my goddamned coat when I *want* to take off my goddamned coat." She frowned. "I suppose that was a little pissy, huh?"

"More than a little."

"Did you ever think that maybe I'm worried about my husband?"

And that was all she needed.

Went absolutely bonkers. Just stood there in her coat with a pound of bacon and a head of lettuce and a big red tomato in her hand and started sobbing.

And I felt like a shit, of course.

If either of us had a right to be pissy, it was her. Not me.

I hugged her as best I could without mashing up our dinner.

A couple of times while she was crying, she said, "Be careful of the tomato."

Which was just about as strange a comment as I might have expected standing here in the dying gray winter day, holding a woman I hardly knew in an apartment I'd never been in before, sad because I was losing those very powers that had always made me a freak, trying to elude the men the President of the United States had dispatched to arrest and maybe even kill me.

"I'm sorry," she said, snuffling up the last of her tears and getting her balance back.

"Look, maybe both of us should just issue blanket apologies to each other and let it go at that."

"Good idea."

"I'm heartily sorry for all the ways I've offended you."

" 'Heartily sorry?' That's from the Act of Contrition."

"Former Catholic."

"Ah." She smiled. "You're not so bad, really."

"Thank you. Neither are you."

"Maybe now would be a good time to go talk to Angela. While I get dinner."

"Just give me the L and the T but leave off the B."

"Smart-ass. And I still can't believe you're a vegetarian."

"Why should some poor little animal have to die when my body doesn't even need what he gives me anyway?"

"God, a true believer."

I tugged her close, still careful of the elements of dinner she was holding in her hands, and kissed her on the forehead.

"How come you did that?"

"Because you're a nice woman. Most of the time."

"Bend your head down here."

"Huh?"

"Bend your head down here."

I bent my head down there.

She kissed me on the forehead. "Now we're even."

The first thing Angie asked me (after telling me how much she hated "Angel") was did I ever see *My Fair Lady*, which gave me an opportunity to sound intellectual because I got to say, "No, but I did see *Pygmalion*, the original George Bernard Shaw play on which it was based."

She didn't look all that impressed, just sort of shrugged and said, "That's sort of how our relationship went."

"Yours and Dr. Finebaum's?"

"Uh-huh."

We sat in a room overlooking the Garden in the foggy distance. We sat in plush blue armchairs, sipped warm ginger ale, and ate prim little sugar cookies that snapped in half at the slightest touch.

"They want to kill him, you know."

"They?"

"The President. The people at NASA. They're all in on it."

"In on what?"

She looked at me a moment, then said, "You know what I'm afraid of?"

"What?"

"That you're one of them."

"One of who?"

"Would you tilt your head away from me."

"Like this?"

"A little more to the right."

"Like this?"

"A little more, even."

"This?"

"Just hold it there."

She was very appealing and very sleek in her mauve ensemble. Appealing and sleek, yes, but I didn't have a clue as to what she was doing.

"I don't see anything."

"What were you looking for?"

"Little flashes of orange. Deep in the eyes."

"And that would mean what exactly?"

"What exactly?" She sipped her ginger ale daintily and said, "It would mean that you're an alien is what it would mean exactly."

"An alien?"

"That's what Dr. Finebaum—Jason—found out. When he first started working with Jack Campbell a few months ago, Campbell could still talk. He hadn't withdrawn as much as he has lately. I guess he told Dr. Finebaum quite a lot about it. Something happened on his last mission—I never did find out what. Anyway, he came down with this rash on the inside of his forearms. Not long after that he started having these strange dreams and hearing strange voices and he was scared. He convinced Jason that there really was something going on. Then the orange lights showed up and he quit telling Dr. Finebaum anything." A little more warm ginger ale. "That's why I wanted to look at your eyes. Make sure you're not one of them."

I didn't know what to say. Although I'd already known some of it, it was a little overwhelming to hear it like that.

She had another cookie, and a little more ginger ale. "The color in their eyes; the rash on the arms; and the gestalt thing—Jason said they were all characteristics of a human who had been taken over by these aliens."

"What's the gestalt thing?"

She shrugged, smiled sadly. "We haven't gotten that far in our *My Fair Lady* thing. Jason has got me reading books like *The Great Gatsby* and listening to composers like Mozart and taking me to art galleries to see the Vermeers and Degases—but he certainly hasn't turned me into a scientist yet. Don't forget, I'm just a girl from the housing projects. I'd still be a hooker if I hadn't met Jason. One of my johns was chasing me and he pulled his car over and told me to get in. It was like a movie—this handsome older man coming out of nowhere to save me. He took me back to his place, and I stayed there for nine days without ever going outside even once. And he listened to me pour my heart out, and I listened to him pour his heart out. I don't think I ever knew anybody who loved his wife as much as Jason did. Anyway, that's how we became such good friends." The sad smile again. "But that doesn't mean I can explain the gestalt thing other than the President is in on it, and every person they add makes them stronger. Jason said it was an exponential thing, and that when they had enough minds they'd be strong enough to reach and link up with others out in space—if there are any others. If that happens, he said, there'll be no stopping them."

"How does it work?"

She shrugged. "It starts with a rash on the inner arms, moves to lights in the eyes, and then, bam, you're one of them. As for how it works, Jason said it's like a virus, but it isn't airborne. Jason said it seems to be spread like a common cold, by coughing and sneezing and kissing. Stuff like that."

Kissing, I thought. Jack Campbell was infected, and Pam had kissed him.

"What about an incubation period?" I asked. "Did he say how long it takes to start affecting a person?"

She shrugged again. "I'm sorry. If he did, I don't remember it."

Damn. But I guess it didn't matter anyway. I already knew time was running out.

"All right. The President's men, they're the ones who've been chasing you?"

She nodded, finished her tea. "They want me to tell them where Jason is. Right now, Jason's the only threat to their whole plan."

"Where is Jason?"

"He didn't tell me where he would be."

I thought of scanning her, seeing if I could pick up anything that way, but I was afraid she'd figure out what I was doing and resent me.

"Why not?"

"Why didn't he tell me where he'd be?"

"Yeah."

"Because he knew they'd come after me. And my knowing would make things dangerous for me."

"I'll bet you could make a good guess, though."

She stared at me a long moment. "I bet I sound pretty crazy, huh? All that alien invasion jazz?"

"Unfortunately, you don't sound crazy at all."

"I have to be careful. About you, I mean. For Jason's sake."

"I understand."

"Let me see your arm."

"Right arm, inside?"

"Right arm, inside."

I took off my sports jacket, unbuttoned my sleeve, turned the inside of my arm toward her.

She clipped on a gooseneck lamp and brought it close, like a doctor examining a mole.

"The stuff I've told you so far, if you're one of them, you'd know all that already."

She took a long red fingernail and moved it around on an area just below the crook of my elbow.

"You look clean."

"Good. Then you'll tell me."

She clipped off the light. "I really don't know. Not for sure, anyway."

"But you sound as if you could make a good guess."

"There's a deserted motel out by Fort McNair—you know where that is?"

"Sure."

"Well, they got six or seven units built, but then the builder's finance guy pulled out and the builder went bankrupt."

"But the six or seven units have lights?"

"Uh-huh. The builder's Jason's second cousin or something like that. The whole place is set back from the road and has this big FOR SALE sign up and it looks completely deserted. Jason could cover the windows with heavy blankets and you'd never be able to see any light from the road. He took me out there one day. It was kind of weird. You ever walk around in a ghost town? A john took me to Arizona once and we spent a day in this old ghost town and I swear to God I heard ghosts calling my name. The john thought I was pretty crazy."

"This sounds like a good lead, Angie. I appreciate it."

"Tell him I love him, all right?"

"Sure."

"I do, too. That's the strange thing. I never really loved anybody before and then I woke up in bed with him one morning—I was with him four, five weeks before he ever even kissed me—and I realized that I was in love with somebody. I cried and he got all bent out of shape, you know how men are when ladies cry, and then he said that he thought that maybe he was in love with me, too, but that he felt real guilty about his wife and all so he wouldn't mention it for a while, loving me and all, he'd just sort of keep it to himself, you know?"

"I appreciate it, Angie."

I stood up and she put out her hand and I took it, silky and graceful and slender it was, and then I went out to the dining area where Pam had dinner ready, two BLTs and one LT.

25

Night came, and with it all the Christmas carols and all the Christmas lights and all the big Christmas displays, and for little kids it was no doubt wonderful, the promise of days off from school, of snowball fights and ice forts and quick scary sled rides, but for adults it was different—more added to the American Express card, forced joviality with in-laws you basically didn't like, and maybe even resenting your own kids a little for all the quick pure joy that they could feel and you couldn't. All the other holidays are for boozy adults—all the New Year's Eves and all the Fourths of July and all the Memorial Days—but Christmas is strictly for kids, and once you get kicked out of that particular club, they never let you back in.

I thought of all these things as Pam and I drove out near Ft. McNair, looking for the still-born motel Angie had told me about. She was driving and doing a damned good job of it given all the snow.

In the darkness of the car, with the *whooshing* heater making both of us a tad groggy and the FM tuned low to a wistful old Boz Scaggs ballad, Pam said, "Could you just read my mind right now—I mean, if I let you?"

"It'd take a while."

"Even if I just sat here and sort of invited you in?"

"Still take some doing."

"Why don't I think of a number between ten and twenty and see if you can guess it?"

"You should work at the University. They love doing stuff like this."

"Try it. C'mon."

Nobody ever quite gets over it, once they know you're an esper, I mean. It scares them a little bit—what if you're having some really embarrassing thoughts and somebody taps into your mind—but more than that if fascinates them.

"All right. Got your number?"

"Got it."

"Forty-three."

She laughed. "Asshole. C'mon. I'm serious."

So I gave it a serious try.

And surprised myself.

True, getting a useful scan takes awhile. But just as in stressful moments you can get images of somebody coming after you, there are times when you effect a mind tap and pick up a few stray bits of information immediately. This was one of them.

"You're not going to believe this."

"Believe what?"

"I picked it up."

"My number?"

"Uh-huh."

"Then tell me."

"Don't start thinking I can do this all the time."

"Or confusing you with Clark Kent or anything."

"Right," I said, as we passed a dark street where white powdered snow blew through the dim light cast by a lone streetlight.

Boz Scaggs was still being wistful and it wasn't helping at all. Every few moments, I'd have memories of my first wife, and how hard and bitter and sapping it had been for both of us at the end.

"So are you going to tell me?"

"Eighteen. You were going to say twelve, but you thought that might be an easier number to guess. So you went with eighteen."

"God."

"That's all you're going to say?"

She looked at me.

"It's kind of spooky," she said, and even

though physically she didn't move an inch, I felt her slide away from me.

"You all right?"

"Yes, fine," she said, but she was staring out the window at the house in the winter gloom, and she didn't sound fine at all.

We had to do a little hiking, parking the car about a quarter mile away on a street where the people were in a bitter competition to see who could have the most splendiferous holiday house. There were so many lights, it was like walking down a street in Vegas.

The motel was made up of three Tudor-style buildings. In the snow-whipped darkness, with the wind crying through the eaves like a prowling ghoul, it had a certain haunted quality, an air of great and utter abandonment. This Poe-like gloom was soon banished by all the graffiti. Dirty words have a way of bringing you right back to gritty reality.

Kids with rocks had smashed out most of the windows. Glass crunched beneath the cushion of snow.

We walked through the first building, me spearing the shadows with my flashlight, and saw the high fine idea that had inspired the motel—here is where the swimming pool would have been, there the big open fireplace; here, the bar, so snug and friendly on lonely rainy nights; there, the game room for the youngsters, and couldn't you just hear them now with their video games?

But the reality remained broken glass on the floor, wind whistling through the smashed windows, and a myriad of dirty words covering the walls.

We spent ten minutes in the first building, and about the same amount of time in the second.

Then it was on to the third, the one closest to the dark woods in back.

I sensed him.

He'd been here.

A shattered image of Finebaum appeared.

"He's been here."

"But he's not here now?"

"I don't think so."

She hurried up the inner stairs ahead of me, slipping on some shards of glass, grasping the rail just in time to keep from falling.

I caught up with her. "Careful."

"He can help my husband. I know he can."

About every half hour, she gave in to panic and it always made me feel sorry for her, and a bit envious of her husband. When this woman loved you, you stayed loved.

"Did you see anything else?"

"Just a kind of blurry photograph of Dr. Finebaum."

"But you definitely sensed that he was here?"

"That he'd been here."

"Let's try the top floor first."

So we did, and in a room in the middle of a long, broad, and very dark hall, we found a room with a space heater, a cot with no box spring and a McDonald's sack sitting in the center of the floor.

And then I found the comb.

It was sitting on the edge of the cot, dropped by accident and forgotten.

In the beam of the flashlight, I saw a few gray hairs in the black plastic teeth.

She looked at the comb, and the careful way I picked it up. "God, do you think it's his?"

"Yes," I said. "It is."

She gave me a look that was hard to read. "Have you ever worked with the police?"

"Only once, and then I wished I hadn't. I found the remains of a ten-year-old girl. I've never been able to forget it. I even have nightmares about it."

She nodded to the comb. "Are you getting any—vibes—or whatever you call it?"

I closed my eyes. Concentrated on the comb. "Water."

"What?"

"Black, choppy water."

"A river?"

"Probably."

I concentrated a little more then opened my eyes. "That's it."

"Just the water?"

"Just the water. I wonder if Dr. Finebaum has a boat."

"We could call the marinas."

There were lots of little harbors within a few hours' drive of Washington, D.C., all with their own little marinas. Calling each of them would be an act of desperation.

I hoped it wouldn't come to that.

"Let's try something else, first. Did you catch that nurse's name?"

"From last night?"

"Right. She seemed like she might be willing to help us."

She gave me the name she had seen on the nurse's uniform.

"Let's go."

"We're done?"

"I don't see him any place, do you?"

"You going to call the nurse?"

"Yes," I said, and led her across the glass-strewn floor. He'd lived here a little while, sort of like a hobo, Finebaum had, but then he'd given it up. I couldn't understand why, given the plush accommodations.

After I told the nurse my name, there was a pause.

"They're looking for you, you know that?"

"Who is?"

"The D.C. Police."

"For what?"

"Murdering some young woman."

"What?"

"They're also looking for Mrs. Campbell."

"For what?"

"Same thing. The murder, I mean."

"We didn't murder anybody."

"I'm just telling you what I heard on the TV in the lounge. All the staff got pretty excited, being that the wife of one of our patients is involved and all."

"You remember her name?"

"The woman you were supposed to have killed?"

"Yeah."

"Angela something."

Even though that was who I suspected had been killed so we could be neatly framed for the murder, I still felt sick when I heard about it. Less than three hours ago, Angie had been an intelligent, appealing young woman. Now. . .

"I need to ask you a question about Dr. Finebaum."

"I really shouldn't even be talking to you."

"Please."

"All right, but then I'm going to hang up because I'm starting to feel guilty."

"We didn't kill anybody."

"I'll take your word for that."

I sighed. But there was no use trying to convince her. No use at all. "Dr. Finebaum, does he have a boat?"

"What kind of boat?"

"Any kind of boat."

"Uh," she said, thinking it over, "no."

"You're sure?"

"But Dr. Lewis does."

"Dr. Lewis?"

"Another psychiatrist here. But he and his wife are in Europe for three months. It's a houseboat. Nice one, too."

"You know where he keeps it?"

"On the Potomac." She thought a moment and then came up with the approximate location.

"Does it have a name?"

" 'Cindy Loo.' Two 'o's. He named it for his daughter."

"I see. Well, I appreciate this."

"I really should call the police and tell them you called me. Because if I don't, I'll feel guilty."

"Call them, then."

"But on the other hand, maybe you really are innocent, so if I called them I'd feel guilty about you and Mrs. Campbell. You understand?"

"Sort of."

"So I guess I won't call them."

"I appreciate that."

"They say she was cut up pretty bad."

Poor Angie, I thought. She died just so the President and his men could make things worse for us.

"You still thinking about Angie?" Pam said thirty-five minutes later, as we headed toward the Potomac.

"Yeah." I couldn't figure out how they'd found her so fast, but I didn't want to mention that to Pam. More than that, I didn't want to think about her kissing Jack, about becoming exposed, about becoming one of them. Most of all, though, I didn't want to wonder if it was already too late. Because if it was, there just wasn't anything I could do.

"So am I." She stared out the window. "Even though Jack was a Marine for eight years, I never quite believed that people could actually just kill each other. In cold blood, I mean. You know, the way Angie was murdered."

"Yeah. I know what you mean."

"I'll bet they're not thinking of her."

"Who?"

"The men who killed her. I'll bet they're not thinking of her at all. You know, how pretty she was or how bright or how she was turning her life around." She started crying just a little bit there behind the wheel as we slowed to stop for a red light. "It's just a shitty world sometimes. Just such a shitty old world."

There wasn't much I could say to that.

26

Pam saw the whipping red emergency lights before I did.

Down in a shallow valley, against a backdrop of bitter black night sky and bitter black Potomac River, three police cars and an ambulance were parked to the right of a long line of houseboats and other river craft.

As we topped the rise, the white-uniformed ambulance people were carefully pushing a stretcher inside the big boxy vehicle.

"God," Pam said, "I wonder what happened."

"Well, there's no way we can go down there and find out. That's for sure."

On the way over, we'd driven around in the back of my apartment house to the garage and exchanged cars. The elderly Italian man who lived downstairs, for whom I'd done a lot of favors, had gone back to the old country for the holidays. We'd borrowed his venerable Ford four-door.

"I'll pull over here," Pam said.

We watched as the ambulance started to pull up the hill, its siren crying into life. I still have to resist the old Catholic school impulse to make the sign of the cross and say a prayer for the person being taken away.

"There's a man walking up the hill," I said. "I'll talk to him."

I got out of the car, stuffed my hands deep in my pockets, felt my cheeks go dead with cold and waited for the middle-aged man in the parka to reach the top of the hill.

"Hi," I said.

He peered out at me like an Eskimo spotting his first white man.

"Hi," he said without even a hint of friendship.

"What happened down there?"

"Why don't you go down and find out?"

I smiled. "Wife and I are celebrating our fifteenth wedding anniversary. Afraid we might have too much alcohol on our breath for the cops." I kept my aw-shucks smile in place.

He relented, at least a little bit. "I watch over those boats for the owners. Some sonofabitch broke into one of them tonight, and it just so happened that there was someone else on board. Don't ask me what the hell he was doing there on a night like this. He sure as hell wasn't going to take her out."

"I saw an ambulance. The guy get hurt?"

"Pretty bad. Don't know if he's gonna make it, in fact. One cop told me he figured the guy wouldn't be alive by the time they got him to the hospital." He shook his head. "Kind of ironic. Guy's a doctor himself. Finebaum. Poor bastard. They really worked him over." He nodded ahead down the long dark road. "Better hurry up. Wife always worries about me when I'm gone a long time. Used to be we never had any violence out this way. Now the goddamned gangs are always dropping bodies out here. Little sons of bitches. I'd like to get my hands on a couple of them."

And with that, he was gone, vanishing quickly into the snow-lashed darkness.

I got back in the car.

"Was it Dr. Finebaum?"

I nodded.

"Is he alive?"

I nodded again. "But maybe not for long."

She raised her head slowly, and looked over at me. "There's nothing we can do, is there?"

"Doesn't seem like it. Not right now, anyway."

"Couldn't we just go to the police?"

I laughed gently. "And tell them what, that our esteemed President is an alien?"

She smiled sadly. "I guess that would sound pretty crazy."

I reached into my pocket, lifted out the small vial of sorahein.

I held it up, waggled it a little.

"Is that sorahein?"

"You know about sorahein?"

"I told you, I did a lot of background checking." She paused. "I couldn't let you take it. It's way too risky."

"We need to know what Dr. Finebaum knows."

"But knowing what that does to people—"

"Some people—"

"But that could be you. There's no need to be heroic."

"Can you think of any other way we can communicate with Dr. Finebaum if he's unconscious?"

"Yes, I know, but—"

"We need a motel room."

"For what?"

"I need to lie down to take this. And then I need you to take care of me for the first hour or so."

"God, I really wish you weren't doing this."

"We don't have much choice."

Then I told her about the Seabrook Inn, which wasn't far from here.

27

Pam got me stretched out on the bed, my pillow all plumped up, and then told me to close my eyes, which I did, and then to relax, which I couldn't.

She had one of those little plastic medicine cups that come with some cough syrups. She put the cup to my lips, tilted my head up, and then poured the sorahein down me.

Didn't take long for the effects to start.

The first thing I felt was a rush of cold through my body. I was starting to freeze. My extremities were completely numb. I heard my teeth literally begin to rattle.

And then

lights
red
yellow

blue

explosion

sound ROARING SOUND

green

playground 1959 Bobby Henderson throwing
me a ball

but when it reaches my hands it becomes the
head of Principal Grant the eyes torn out the
mouth vomiting blood

and

sound ROARING SOUND

/I am running down a long corridor and a
monster of some kind is after me—he has killed
my parents and now, dripping blood, is coming
after me/I am eight years old/I cry out for my
mother and father even though I know they
cannot answer me/And then I am in a dark
closet hiding/I am shivering I have to go to the
bathroom very badly/I give up control of my
bladder and feel warm urine spread across my
crotch; even though my life is in danger and
even though I'm only eight, I'm ashamed/I can
smell the monster on the other side of the
door/I want to puke/His talons rip through
the wood of the closet door/He begins to rip the
door apart in big chunks that he hurls angrily

over his shoulder/And then I see him and who he is—a teenage boy named Mike who one day asked me to do something dirty with him and when I refused and ran away, he came after me like now/Mike is coming into the closet now and I am screaming screaming/Huddling deep against the shadowy back wall of the closet please no oh god please no mommy and daddy stop him please stop him and

/A warm April evening when I follow them to Freedom Plaza, their usual rendezvous spot/Am behind a chinaberry tree when he takes her in his arms and kisses her/And then I begin to hear them and I do not want to hear them/But my esper powers are such that I am beginning to get a good solid scan on them and so I can hear them

—He wanted to make love to me last night. But I don't want him to touch me any more.

—You need to tell him. Tonight.

—I'm afraid of him. Those powers he has—

—He can read minds, darling. So what? That's nothing to be afraid of.

—But I keep thinking—there was that CIA experiment—when those men learned how to explode things with just their minds—

—And what happened to them? They all killed themselves. (Laugh) Darling, if he had that kind of power, he wouldn't be here today.

—He just sits in the living room every night

with the lights out listening to those depressing records of his, all those jazz things—

——As soon as you tell him, darling, you can move out.

(Embracing)

—Oh, I want you inside me tonight, David. Let's go back to your car. Thank God you've got that big Buick.

—(Laughs) It'll be like high school, darling.

—I just want you inside me. That's all I care about.

/I am in a tower of some sort in a circular room with a wraparound window and there in a cot lies my father dying and I hold his hand and plead with him not to die and yet there before me his hair becomes white and his face becomes mummified and when his jaws fall open a gnarled slimy hand comes up from his throat and the world is suddenly a storm lightning and thunder crashing blinding and deafening me the wraparound window smashing into a million bits of glass and the rain pouring in but it is not rain it is blood and

"Can you say your name?"

"What?"

"Tell me your name."

"I don't know my name."

"Do you know who I am?"

"No."

"I'm your friend."

"I don't have any friends."

"You've taken a drug."

"What?"

"A drug called sorahein."

"What's that pounding?"

"You just screamed."

"I just screamed?"

"Yes."

"When?"

"Just now."

"I didn't hear myself scream."

"No, but the people in the room next to ours did. They've been banging on the wall for the past hour or so."

"Who am I?"

silence SILENCE

ROARING SILENCE

"Hurry."

"What?"

"Hurry. We have to get out of here."

"Here?"

"This motel room. They've called the police. Hurry now."

"What happened?"

"You—got angry, I guess."

*She is half-dragging me into the bathroom and for
the first time I become conscious enough to see.*

*The room is a mess, two chairs smashed, two
lamps overturned, bureau drawers hurled across
one of the beds.*

*I stagger into the bathroom, turn on the cold
water, begin to splash my face, and work the cold
water into my eyes.*

*And then I see her in the mirror. Blood on the
corner of her mouth. A bruise on her cheek.
Clothes torn.*

"Hurry," *she says.*

Snow. Night. Freezing leather car seats.

*She turns the ignition on. Motor doesn't fire
properly.*

"Shit," *she says.*

Sirens now. Closer.

She tries the motor again.

This time it catches.

Sirens. Closercloser.

"Roll your window down."

"What?"

"Your window. Roll it down. Maybe it'll help."

"Help?"

"Help you wake up."

"Oh."
I roll my window down.

night houses dark narrow icy streets hurry hurry
fastfast
window rolled down
freezing whistling wind
"does that help?"
"huh?"
"is that waking you up?" she says.
"oh, yeah, yeah it is."
is that really me speaking?
is there really a "me" am i anything more than
an antenna picking up sensory data cold distant
sirens coldCOLD

she goes away comes back
"try this."
"huh?"
"try this."
i try this.
"what is it?"
"coffee?"
"oh."
scalding hot. paper cup even hotter on my fin-
gers as wind whistles through open window.

Sometime much later, I said, "I need to take
a pee."

Pam looked over at me and smiled. "Welcome back."

"How long have I been—gone?"

"Six hours."

"God, it was supposed to be over in an hour. Do I remember something about a motel room?"

"Yes, and I'll bet the motel remembers something about you, too."

This was like being forced to remember drunken blackouts during which you did some pretty horrendous things. There had been a two-or three-minute period far back there when my senses sang with great swelling power—a symphony that made me feel like a superman— but darkness came quickly and then I was cold and scared and lost.

"I was bad?"

And then I flashed on the room. "I broke up the furniture, right?"

"Right."

"And I—hit you?"

"Not on purpose. I was trying to stop you from smashing everything up. You just shoved me to get me out of the way. But your elbow caught me on the cheek and the mouth. You've got pretty tough elbows."

We were parked in an alley half a block away from the hospital.

"I'm sorry."

"I'll survive," she said. "But now we really need to talk to Dr. Finebaum. Before you took your little jaunt, you said you had a plan."

"Oh, right," I said, but it was five minutes before I remembered it.

28

Just before five that morning, on the sixth floor of St. Elizabeth's Hospital, the door beneath a softly glowing EXIT sign opened and through it came a nurse and an orderly.

They looked both ways down the still and shadowy hallway and then began walking crisply in an easterly direction toward a room outside of which sat a uniformed policeman, who was reading a magazine in very bad light.

When he heard the duo coming, he looked up and nodded hello. He was probably grateful for company. A hospital corridor wasn't the most exciting place in the best of circumstances—at night, it was dark, silent, and maybe even a little bit eerie, so many souls in this building ready to jump across the line into eternity.

The nurse and the orderly reached him, greeted him in the sort of stage whisper that was proper to the occasion, and then the nurse leaned forward no more than three or four inches and drove the hypodermic needle deep into the officer's right arm.

He reared up from his chair, a chunky man with a melancholy face, and tried to cry out, but it was already too late. The cry died in his throat. He smelled of sweat and sleepiness.

The intern grabbed the officer underneath the arms and dragged him into the room that was being guarded. The intern found a large closet and propped the officer up inside, making him as comfortable as possible. He also checked his pulse and his breathing. Everything seemed fine, given the shock the man had just received.

The intern closed the door and moved quickly back to the shiny waxed corridor where the nurse had been keeping watch.

They whispered a few more words and then the intern went back into the room.

That was how I got into Dr. Finebaum's room so I could probe him.

The analogy of a bad acid trip, for my first brush with sorahein, kept on working just fine. The one and only time I'd dropped acid, I'd spent days being besieged by sensory data that was too colorful, too loud, or too sweet or too fetid to the nose and taste system.

As I leaned over Dr. Finebaum's bed, the only light in the room the silver moonlight against the closed drapes, I was starting to get another case of the too-muches. His ragged breathing was like drums in my head; the pus and poisons of his wounds clogged my nose; and the faint green light of the EEG burned into my eyes like sunspots.

Earlier, while we were stealing the uniforms that would allow us to walk through the hospital, I'd noticed this starting to happen. Nobody at the University had warned me about it.

But even with the drug, the probe was not easy.

I spent the first fifteen minutes looking down at Dr. Finebaum and feeling sorry for him. Difficult to believe he'd lived through a beating that had broken both his arms, one of his legs and given him a very serious concussion. They'd obviously left him for dead, the President's men had, but by now they'd likely heard the bad news that he'd survived.

Finally, I started scanning, picking up the random word and the sentence fragment and the sudden swooping emotion (pain, rage, joy, pleasure, they can all overwhelm you when you're scanning, even if you don't know what they refer to—the feeling itself is enough).

I saw some of the beating he'd taken: I didn't recognize either of the men. They looked to be pretty much what you might expect government thugs to look like, good preppy tweed sport jackets to offset the brass knuckles. They wanted to

know what he'd learned from Jack Campbell—
and what he'd done with his notes. After a time,
frustrated, the poor dears, they'd gotten a little
overzealous. One of them broke Finebaum's nose
and that looked like so much fun that the other
one broke one of Finebaum's ribs. And so on.
Then, convinced that he was dead, they fled.

And then it happened.

A true probe.

I slipped inside his mind like a surgical blade
deftly entering a body.

Now it was my turn to feel great swooping
joy. It had been years—maybe as many as
eight—since I'd probed anybody with this kind
of range or depth.

I was somebody again.

Dr. Jason Finebaum's story

Several months ago a patient arrived at
the hospital under a cloud of secrecy. Hastings House has done work for the government before—all very hush-hush—so we
didn't really expect anything out of the ordinary.

We were wrong.

The patient's name was Captain Jack
Campbell, and he had recently returned
from a mission in space. The government
wanted to know if Jack had suffered some

kind of trauma up there, something that would account for his odd behavior.

At the start, physical observation yielded far more than any of the standard mental tests.

—I noticed three different rashes on different parts of his body. The rashes resembled ***Borrelia burgorferi,*** or Lyme disease. But lab analysis could not give me an identification.

—A curious keening sound during the REM portions of Jack's sleep. I even brought in a specialist, but he could not remember hearing this sound in any of his clinical tests with students. He suggested that the keening sound, which reminded him of a dolphin's sound, might be some kind of communication. He noted that the sounds I played him on the tape resembled repeated words.

—An orangish light deep in the pupils of his eyes. At first, I didn't believe this, thought I must be imagining things. But I wasn't. I even managed to get a fairly decent videotape of Jack sitting in a chair with his eyes open and the orangish light flickering deep in his eyes.

—The strange symbols Jack drew on the walls of his room. They made no sense to anybody who saw them. One nurse said they reminded her of the "nonsense lines"

that children make when they're first learning manual dexterity with crayons. But
there was a recurring pattern, the same
symbols over and over.

—Jack's response, after a few months, to
the various experimental "truth" serums I'd
been developing for a group pf psychiatrists
who regularly dealt with severely repressed
patients.

It was at this point that I requested medical histories and recent observations of all
the astronauts who had accompanied
"Cap'n Jack" on his last mission. As this involved several foreign countries, I expected
a moderate wait. But what happened was
that the authorities told me, in no uncertain
terms, that I was to confine my investigations to the patient at hand.

Needless to say, this significantly ham-
pered my study, but having worked with the
government before I was hardly surprised. I
was also hardly defeated.

In the past, when faced with similar situations, I have relied on the services of a
man named Callahan, a rather shadowy
figure who worked for hire as a computer
hacker. He had the talent to access most of
the government's files—including some
highly classified documents for some agencies I've never even heard of—and so I
turned to him for help.

Well, Callahan was able to get the records of the astronauts, too. Took him two weeks and cost me five thousand dollars of my own money, but it was worth it because I found a great deal of useful information— and I also found evidence that the highest officials in the land wanted the astronauts' medical records kept hidden.

A Dr. Carleton Wright, a NASA staffer, worked on most of the astronauts before and after their return from space.

Like me, he noted:

—a rash resembling Lyme disease
—pulsating points of orange light in their eyes
—sluggish vital signs, suggesting a critical deterioration
—an irascibility not previously noted

These observations took Dr. Wright to the highest levels of NASA. Six days following this meeting, Dr. Wright's home caught on fire and he died in the flames.

Two other physicians took his place, but they were only allowed to work on the American astronauts. No mention of any physical peculiarities ever appeared in any of their reports.

It was time for me to do a little detective work on my own. Here are some of the things I learned:

—Captain Linda Baxter, one of Cap'n Jack's colleagues on his last mission, showed this same rash and these same orange lights for the first three days after returning to Earth.

—Six days later, President Haskins held a welcoming ceremony for all the returning astronauts. Only Cap'n Jack Campbell did not attend.

—Three weeks after the ceremony, the President's physician was killed in a mysterious small-plane crash.

—Eight weeks later, more than half the President's Cabinet had been observed with a faint rash on their inner forearms.

After I had worked with Jack for several weeks, I began to compare his medical history with those of the other astronauts. Discounting such differences as gender (like the fact that Captain Baxter had had a hysterectomy some eight years ago), I was unable to find anything that might indicate why he was having problems, while all the others appeared to have recovered from the rash and the lights. Which is to say, while I was unable to learn whether these symptoms had ever gone away, I was unable to find any reports of the same kind of aberrant behavior Jack was demonstrating.

The only thing I found was the tattoo Jack reported getting shortly before leaving on his last mission. This did not appear to be significant, but as I had no other leads, I decided to investigate it.

I did some reading on tattoos. Usually, for a particularly heavy tattoo, cadmium is used. This is an intense yellow pigment which takes on the color of deep red when it is worked beneath the epidermis. The reputation of tattoos as being dangerous to receive probably comes from this. Introduce too much cadmium at any one point into the human system and you have a very sick person on your hands. The person might even go into shock and die.

Some of Jack's symptoms resembled systemic shock; others—well, others I'd simply never heard of before. So I took another look at that rash, the one that so resembled Lyme disease. What I found was both wondrous and terrifying.

The rash was the result of a virus—an alien virus, that appeared to have been tailored to work on our genetic material. I say "appeared to have been tailored" because of the sophistication of its attack. Also, its effects are not consonant with naturally-occurring viruses found here on Earth. The alterations in the genetic material appear to strip the individuality from those exposed, and make them a part of a collective consciousness.

My conclusions—which I checked and

rechecked more than a dozen times—were that Earth had been exposed to the opening stages of an alien invasion, and that the President of the United States had become one of its first victims.

It appeared that the cadmium inhibited the virus, and that was why Cap'n Jack Campbell was experiencing those symptoms. The virus was attempting to influence his DNA, and the cadmium was interfering with this process. His entire body had essentially become a battleground, and as with many villages in Vietnam, the very ground being fought over was being destroyed by the war.

It was about this time that I realized that Callahan had vanished. Shortly after that, I noticed signs that I was being watched. This put an end to my investigations, so I was never able to conduct my next experiment, which was to have been the administering of a large dose of cadmium to Captain Jack Campbell. It is my belief that a large enough dose—a dose that would, in short, kill an uninfected human—may be sufficient to destroy the invading virus.

I am afraid of what I must do, but my task is clear and I must not fail.

I have sent two samples of the virus out to colleagues of mine. Knowing I was being watched, and knowing they would expect such a thing from me, I called upon the services of my good friend, Colonel Thomas Rodham, to conduct a study of one of the tissue samples and some patient files. I selected Colonel Rodham, even though he and I have been friends for a long time, not only because he was a logical choice, but because he told me not long ago that he has been diagnosed with pancreatic cancer. The disease was too far along for them to treat.

I wish that this knowledge could make my choice easier, for I know that I sent my friend out to die. It does not. My only hope is that he will not have died in vain.

I also sent a sample, along with a complete set of my notes, conclusions, and speculations, to a genetic research lab I know of. I have not been in contact with them since, for fear of exposing them, but I've determined that they will require a minimum of three months to develop a vaccine against this alien plague.

The problem is, we don't have three months. This alien collective controls our President, and through him all the law enforcement agencies of our country. To stop this virus, or even to slow its spread, we must regain control of our government.

And that is why I say my task is clear, yet frightening, for I must undertake to kill the President of the United States.

I have resolved to attempt this, at any

rate. My studies show that if the organism is allowed to acquire more members, it will soon reach a critical point and become unstoppable by any means short of total nuclear annihilation.

I have acquired an amount of cadmium, and have even started preparations for fashioning this into a weapon. It took four days of trial and error to do what I needed to—aided considerably by a gunsmith who spat streams of tobacco into a reeking metal wastebasket the entire time I was in his workshop—and then it was just a matter of saying good-bye to Angie (who, in my way, I've fallen in love with) and then hiding out while I prepared myself to become what I needed to become to do my duty properly.

I've never been one for flag-waving—in fact, I downright distrust most flag-wavers—but I knew that no matter how terrible I found the task ahead, I had to do it for the sake of my country and my species.

What choice did I have?

My probe ended there. Apparently, Finebaum never had a chance to carry through on his plan.

"Hurry," Pam said moments later, "somebody's coming."

We couldn't afford to get caught. Not now.

I turned away from Dr. Finebaum, feeling sorry as hell for him and wishing there were something I could do for him, and quickly headed for the door.

By now, the hospital was coming alive for the morning. Soft gongs rang out in some arcane language; food carts rattled with breakfast; and patients were turning on lights, radios, and televisions.

As I reached the door, I saw a burly uniformed cop walking toward us.

We turned and started away in the opposite direction, but he was quicker than his size would indicate.

In seconds I could smell his aftershave. I was still getting contact highs from the sorahein I'd taken.

"Where's McCarthy?"

Pam had stayed cooler than I had. "The police officer stationed at the door?"

"Yeah." He looked us over suspiciously. I noticed that the heel of his hand rested on the handle of his 9-mm Glock semiautomatic. These days, cops had to be prepared for real warfare.

"Said he wasn't feeling well," Pam said calmly. "He's in the bathroom." She nodded to the dark interior of Dr. Finebaum's room.

"Oh."

"He'll be right out."

Some of the suspicion drained from the cop's eyes. "Just seemed kind of weird. I expected him to be sitting there, I guess." He nodded to the empty chair.

Pam said, "Don't you have surgery in a few mintues, Dr. Highsmith?"

I nodded. "Yes, I do."

"I'm scheduled for the same operation. I'll walk down with you." She looked at the cop. "Tell Officer McCarthy that I hope he's feeling better. He seems like a very nice man."

"He is," the cop said. "He's a great guy."

He went over and sat down in the empty chair.

If he thought there was anything strange about us taking the fire stairs instead of an elevator, he didn't let on.

Ten frantic minutes later, we were climbing inside Pam's car, still in our hospital whites, our street clothes piled in the back.

Breathlessly, and at the same time firing up the ignition, Pam said, "Now what?"

"Now I've got a job to do."

"What job?"

I looked at her quite seriously and said, "I guess I have to assassinate the President of the United States."

"Are you serious?"

"How else do we get rid of the alien?"

She didn't say anything for a long time. Then she said, "My God, you really do have to kill him, don't you?"

29

December 3

In the control room, everything seemed normal.
Jacobs was in her acceleration couch, monitor-
ing the flow of data from her controls. Varnov,
one of the two Russians, who looked like a
welder but was actually an astrophysicist with a
medical degree and extremely gentle hands,
was going over the printouts of some earlier
runs on the samples they'd taken from the
comet. Nablokov, the other Russian, was as-
sisting him. Martinelle, the French biochemist,
was doing something with the video camera up
in the corner.

Miriam Goldmann was the only one missing.
Wendy looked around, visions of the bloody rag
still vivid in her mind, but the Israeli was nowhere to be seen.

"Where—" she said, but that was as far as
she got.

As soon as she spoke, all three men turned to face her. As one, they all reached out and touched their inner forearms, and then they all smiled.

It was eerie, almost as though they'd formed a dance troupe in her absence. Confused, Wendy turned to Colonel Jacobs, and that was when she saw it: the flash of orange light in the Colonel's eyes.

She started to turn away, started to ask a question, started to do anything to try to make sense of what was happening, but before she could Varnov was standing before her.

"Feodor," she said. "What's—"

He reached out his gentle hands and touched her face, startling her into silence. He had black hair, and eyes so blue they looked like the oceans of Earth as seen from space.

Wendy looked into his eyes, and there was that same orange light. Not as bright as the one she'd seen in the Colonel's, but it was there, and it was definitely not a reflection.

"What—" she said.

Feodor leaned forward, bringing his lips lightly against her own.

For a moment Wendy didn't react. Then, as she felt herself starting to relax, she smelled that same musky odor coming from Feodor. She knew, then, what it was, and what had happened.

The bloody rag. Miriam's absence from the

control room. The smell of sex that clung to Feodor like a stain.

She stiffened, and tried to pull away, but Feodor's gentle hands tightened upon her face, and suddenly his grip was not so gentle. She brought a knee up between his legs, but he blocked it with his thigh. She threw a vicious punch at the side of his face, but he blocked it with his shoulder. And all the while he continued to kiss her, gently, lovingly.

And then the kiss turned ugly. All at once his tongue was in her mouth, and Wendy rebelled. Without thinking, she did the only thing she could: she bit down, hard.

For a moment nothing happened, and then he drew back slowly, a smile upon his face. Blood was running down his chin. She could taste it in her mouth, and even though she spat it out in his face, she couldn't get rid of it all.

And then, for the first time since she'd entered the control room, he spoke.

"Welcome, Wendy," he said. "It's all right now. Soon you will understand."

She looked at him, looked at the others, all of them motionless, watching, watching, and then she turned back to him and slammed a hard right into his jaw. He flew backward, the force of her blow driving him into the ceiling, but all the while he just grinned.

Then she turned and fled back out the hatch.

THREE

30

In the morning light, in the bitter cold, the motel construction site was robbed of all its eerie moonlit mystery. Now it was just raw concrete and steel, and it looked like exactly what it was, a dream undone by haste and greed. The snow was yellow in places from animal piss, and every twenty yards or so I'd step on the brown nuggets left by rabbits and dogs. Somebody had left a perfectly good hammer behind and now it was rusted. I paused to brush the snow off it and then stood a moment while the wind came howling between the half-built walls. I thought of Dr. Finebaum hiding out in the next building, in the freezing winter night, and how cold and lonely and frightening it must have been. Even with sunlight, even with blue sky, this section of the construction, like a tumbled-down Mayan temple, gave me a feeling of alienness—the same feeling I'd had when I probed Jack Campbell.

Pam waited in the car, as the lookout.

When I got to Finebaum's building, I went up two flights of wooden steps slick with snow. Floors two and three had been pretty much finished. In the hall of floor two, I started rubbing my hands and then touching my nose to take the freeze off. It felt good to be inside and out of the wind.

The cigarette butt lay on the floor two feet from the door to Dr. Finebaum's room. It was a filter tip. I stooped down and picked it up. The tobacco was still fresh and moist, which meant that the butt hadn't been here very long.

I took my Walther from inside my belt, eased up to the door, and listened.

Wind, mostly, vast crying midwestern wind that would race from city to farmland as it whipped up snow devils and turned cornfields into tundras.

I eased closer, my Walther ready. I scanned for an image but got nothing especially useful.

Somebody inside. Moving things around.

I wouldn't have long, seconds at most, to spring any kind of surprise.

I took a deep deep breath, gripped the doorknob, and flung the door inward.

She was screaming by the time I crossed the threshold, a very attractive young woman bundled up in fashionable and expensive winter clothes.

She had been lifting up the head of the mattress and groping around on the floor to see if Dr. Finebaum had hidden anything there.

She dropped the mattress, stood up, and made a great and obvious attempt to compose herself.

"Is that real?"

"The Walther?"

She nodded.

"Of course it's real."

"It makes me very nervous."

"Right now, I don't care if it makes you nervous. Right now, I want to know who you are and what you're doing here."

"I could ask you the same thing, you know." She sounded scared and vulnerable, which made her seem awfully young. "Dr. Finebaum's my uncle."

"Oh?"

"We've been worried about him."

" 'We' being who exactly?"

"My mother and I. His sister."

"How did you know to look here?"

"He told my mother about this—place. He didn't want to, but she made him." She shrugged. "She's a couple of years older than he is and she's always kind of bossed him around, you know?"

She sounded younger all the time. I felt corny standing there with such a big gun aimed at such a small young woman, but I wasn't in the mood for risks.

"You're him, aren't you?"

"Him?"

"The man the police are looking for."

"I guess I am."

"Did you really kill that woman?"

"No."

"I wondered." She gave a tiny shrug. "You don't look like somebody who'd do that."

I smiled. "Not all crazy people look like Charles Manson. In fact, they'd do society a favor if they *did* look like Charles Manson. You have to be careful."

Now she smiled. "That's sweet."

"What is?"

"You know, kind of giving me advice. I always missed not having a father. He died in Vietnam, my dad, I mean."

"I'm sorry."

And for a moment we just stood there, two uneasy strangers in a pitiful little room that resembled the den of some desperate animal. Except for the McDonald's sack. As far as I know, nobody in the animal kingdom eats Big Macs.

"What're you looking for?"

"What?"

And then the sorahein kicked in and I knew that I wasn't looking at an appealing young woman at all. I was looking at a carefully and craftily contrived mask.

"You know who I am, don't you?" she said.

"Maybe 'what' is more appropriate than 'who.'"

"Would you like to make love?"

And right there, in the middle of the cold, cold room, she dropped her coat and took off her shirt. She wasn't wearing anything beneath it.

An orange light flared deep within her blue, blue eyes, and in spite of myself, in spite of all I knew, I felt a wave of desire wash over me.

That desire frightened me more than anything else I'd felt in the last few days, because it had not come from within me. It had been forced on me by an outside force, and yet it was almost too powerful to ignore.

I thought of Jack's memories, of how they'd had to rape him in order to infect him, and I compared that with what I was feeling right then. I knew, then, that the collective had indeed grown powerful, and that Dr. Finebaum had been right. If it grew too strong, there would be no way to stop it.

She slipped off her skirt and panties and stood before me, naked, offering herself to me. "Come to me, Michael," she said, her voice soft and low and compelling. "Come to me, and I promise you an end to empty nights, an end to your pain and your loneliness, an end to your despair. Come to me, Michael, and find peace." And she took a step forward, reaching out her left hand toward me.

I did the only thing I could: I pulled the trigger, sending a bullet into the very dark center of her very blue left eye.

The force of the shot lifted her a few inches from the cold concrete floor and threw her backward into the wall, where her brain was already sprayed.

I had just run out of time. The alien knew I was aware of it and that I knew how strong it had grown. It would stop at nothing to kill me, or to make me merge with it. I rushed into the closet, looking for what Dr. Finebaum's mind had described to me.

It was all just where he said it would be, taped to the inside of the closet wall, accessed through a hole that looked as if one of the workers had accidentally bumped it with something heavy, everything including an eight-ounce brown bottle marked CADMIUM in longhand.

I took a last look at the young woman—a sudden sorrow for her settling upon me like a great weight—and then hurried back to Pam.

31

"What's that?"

"A gun," I said.

"I know it's a gun. What kind?"

"It's a Smith and Wesson 9-mm automatic that's been modified to single-shot operation."

"It belonged to Dr. Finebaum?"

"Right. And so did these."

"Bullets?"

"Special bullets."

"Why special?"

"He hollowed them out and then put cadmium into them. And they're called subsonic—slower than the speed of sound so they won't make a boom."

"The chemical from Jack's tattoo?"

"Right."

"And so when the President is shot with these—"

"He dies."

"And so does the man who shoots him."

"You want me to sound noble and tell you about the fate of our whole species?"

"There're a lot of other people I'd rather see die than you."

"I'll take that as a compliment."

"You know what I mean."

"Got to be done. And anyway, the way I've got it figured out, I may escape."

"How?"

"See this?"

"What is it?"

"A silencer. Dr. Finebaum hoped he'd escape, too."

"Do those things really work?"

"Well, between the subsonic bullets and the silencer, this is going to be an awfully quiet gun. About all you'd be able to hear is the action clicking."

"I don't know anything about guns, and I'm not sure I want to, either. Anyway, how are you going to escape when he's got all these people standing around him?"

"He won't have anybody standing around him, if things work out."

"What things?"

"Remember Sterling Florist?"

"Sterling Flor— You mean that truck that was ahead of us going through the gates at the White House?"

"Right." I wiped sweat from my forehead. "Could you turn that heater down a little bit?"

"I thought you were cold."

"Not anymore."

She turned down the heater. "What about Sterling Florist?"

"We're going to have an accident with that truck."

"What?"

"I noticed the direction it came from. It came over from E Street."

"You're losing me."

"Remember the guard said that the Sterling truck was there every morning at 10:15 promptly?"

"Right."

"Well, about 10:05, two or three blocks away, we're going to have an accident with the truck." I shivered. "Could I get you to turn the heat up again? It's the sorahein. I'm losing a lot of the contact high stuff—all the bright colors and all the easy scans I was getting—but I've really got a problem with my thermostat. I go from freezing to burning up in just a few minutes."

"This won't work. It really won't. They'll find you and they'll kill you."

I smiled. "Are you going to step on the one big heroic moment of my entire life?"

"I know you're scared. You just won't let on."

I leaned over and touched her softly on the

cheek, something I'd been wanting to do for several hours. "You're a hell of a nice woman, you know that?"

"They'll kill you. They really will."

I nodded to the dashboard clock. "C'mon, we've got to get ready to rear-end somebody in twenty-five minutes."

She nodded and turned back to her driving. We'd reached a busier area, and the press of traffic was claiming more of her attention.

I pulled the small brown bottle of pills from my pocket. Looking at my watch had reminded me that I hadn't taken my vitamins yet today. The way things were shaping up, even with the sorahein, I was going to need all the help I could get.

I unscrewed the cap, shook a couple of the gelatin capsules out into my palm, and froze. The sorahein had kicked in again, just for a moment, and I'd picked up something.

Pam noticed my reaction and asked, "What's up?"

"These," I told her. "I used to work for the government, a long time ago. I don't anymore—not really, anyway. I mean, I guess it's not unlikely that the government funds the lab at the University where I work, but I don't work for the government. Not like I used to."

She nodded, still concentrating on her driving. "And?"

"And I guess they don't want freelancers running around with my kind of power." I showed her the pills. "These are supposed to be vitamins, to help me maintain my abilities as I get older."

She looked at them, then up at me, then back at the traffic. "And they're not?"

"No, they're not. I just picked up a flash from them. They've been shielded, but with the sorahein I was able to learn that these actually function as a sort of anti-sorahein. In other words, they suppress my powers, rather than enhancing them."

She shrugged. "So don't take them."

"Thanks for the advice."

But she was too caught up in her driving to rise to the bait.

I was tempted to throw the pills out the window, but there was something I needed to do first. I thought of how they'd been shielded, and about the gray envelope that also rode in my pocket.

Somehow, someone had figured out a way to shield things from psychic abilities, and I needed to know how to do that. Not because of the alien, but because, having seen what my own government was capable of, I now understood how they'd been able to follow Pam and me so easily. They had another telepath working with them, someone who was tapping into one of us and learning our every move.

And it was time to put a stop to that.

Looking at the two little pills in my hand, I reached once more for the calm stillness within me.

It didn't take long. It turned out that the block was a fairly simple adaptation of the unconscious shield most of us were already capable of. I just hadn't known it could be projected onto inanimate objects. Now that I did, well, I thought I could maybe do something similar.

While Pam brought us ever closer to the White House, I reached into myself for the strength to put up a solid shield around both of us. I doubted that they'd had someone reading us constantly—that would take an awful lot of energy, and I didn't think they could have more than one or two telepaths working with them. Which meant that there was still a chance that they didn't know about our plan.

At any rate, I had to hope so. It was the only plan we had, and there was no time to come up with a new one.

32

At 10:01, the Sterling truck had not yet appeared. Nor at 10:02. Nor at 10:03.

The day before Christmas, the snowy streets were crowded with chilly customers hurrying in and out of stores. Salvation Army Santa Clauses rang their bells on into oblivion. Speakers played warbly old Christmas records, including my favorite, "The Christmas Song" by Nat King Cole. This wasn't a time to get sentimental and yet I was—sentimental for how simple and uncomplicated my life used to be before I learned, in high school, about my powers—powers I hadn't asked for, powers I'm not sure I even wanted back then. But now I wanted even more powers. I wanted to be notable, somebody, and only with my powers did I have a chance. Otherwise, given my somewhat haphazard education, you'd see me behind the counter at McDonald's.

"What happens if they take a different route today?"

"They won't," I said.

"What makes you so sure?"

"Faith."

"I see."

"One of us has to have some."

"I just keep thinking about poor Jack. You know, caught between being a normal human being and—"

"There it is."

"Where?"

"Far end of the block."

She looked left then right.

"I don't see it."

"Coming toward us. Behind that big red truck."

"Oh. Right."

"You remember what you have to do?"

"Yes, but first I have to squeeze in behind him. And the traffic's bumper-to-bumper."

"We'll make it."

She looked over at me and laughed. "Have you been listening to inspirational tapes or something?"

"I just figure that since everything else has gone to shit, he owes us one."

"He?"

"God or whoever."

"Ah."

"Get ready."

"I am ready, thank you."

I'd forgotten that she hated to be told anything about her driving.

The traffic was a long caravan of shiny new cars and the sad rusty ones of the underclass, all packing gifts meant to inspire the Christmas Eve optimism that gets harder to feel with each passing year. Rich or poor, the world takes its toll on us all.

"Now!" she said, and aimed the car like a weapon at a gap of no more than two feet, a gap separating the read end of the blue STERLING FLORIST panel truck and the red chopped-channeled-louvered monstrosity that had once been a 1955 Chevrolet but that had been converted into a street rod of fearsome visage. Like most large cities, the D.C. streets had lately become the scene of too many nighttime drag races. More than fifty innocent pedestrians had been killed in the past year. Remember what I said about Christmas Eve optimism?

She made it.

The racer didn't want any part of his car damaged, so he reluctantly hit his breaks and let Pam sneak in between himself and the panel truck.

He gave us, in sequence, his horn, his scowl, and his finger as Pam pulled into the lane and tooled the steering wheel around so that our tires would run straight.

"You just made a friend," I said.

"He'll survive. Where do we have this accident, anyway?"

"Next block. You'll have to slow down to put some room between us and the truck."

She sighed. "It really pisses me off when you tell me how to drive. You think I can't stage a goddamned accident?"

"I'm sorry. I forgot."

Behind us, the racer revved his motor up so that it was even louder than the massive audio speakers he carried, and that was no small feat.

The light changed, and our lane of vehicles crept forward.

"I sorry I snapped at you," she said.

"I hate backseat drivers myself. I had it coming."

"That's nice of you to say."

"You really are a hell of a nice woman."

I gave her hand a sweet little squeeze. And she gave me a sweet little squeeze right back.

"How's your head?"

I shrugged. "Getting back to normal, I think. But there's this distant kind of buzzing. Like a humming in your ear."

"I hate that. That kind of humming, I mean."

"So do I. I just wish I knew what it meant."

"Probably just means you're still feeling the effects of the sorahein."

"I suppose."

"Damn," she said.

We were now near the next corner. The light was changing. The panel truck would have time to cross the intersection, but we wouldn't.

She floored it. We fishtailed, but she held the car true, and we shot across the intersection and came right up behind the panel truck.

There were the satisfying sounds of our bumper colliding with his rear end and then, faintly, the tinkle of his taillight shattering into jagged red pieces.

"Good?" she said.

"Great. Let's go."

She was out of the car in moments, putting on the face of a distraught suburban housewife whose day had been ruined by causing a silly accident.

She was all gushy apology and penitence.

The driver, a mousy little guy, was, by contrast, quick anger and head-shaking weariness.

They met at the exact spot where her bumper and his rear fender had conjoined.

I didn't hear the rest of it, couldn't, because I was hurrying around the far side of his truck, opening the blessedly unlocked passenger door, and crawling into the back where I hid between festooning floral arrangements meant for the White House and a few nearby funeral homes.

The smell was almost gagging.

The truck was freezing.

I waited.

* * *

A few frozen minutes later, the driver got back in the truck and slammed the door hard enough to make all of his flower arrangements wiggle.

"Stupid bitch," he said. "Mr. Runyon'll blame me for sure."

I suppose most of us do a lot more talking to ourselves than we'd want to admit, but it's still pretty embarrassing to listen to somebody do it because they always sound a little crazy—even if you just wrapped up your own conversation with yourself.

He fired up the engine.

"Stupid bitch."

The truck jerked ahead a few feet.

I leaned forward, pushing through a funeral display that would have made a Pharaoh jealous, and applied the edge of the cold steel to the back of his neck.

"God!" he said. "Don't shoot me, please! We haven't even finished paying for the new furniture I bought the old lady for an anniversary present."

Calling her the "old lady" sort of spoiled this touching moment for me.

"I know where you're headed right now, and I want you to get me inside."

"No, way, man, are you crazy?"

"You don't seem to understand. If you don't help me, I'll kill you."

I wanted to sound as tough as possible. I didn't have a whole lot of time for an argument.

"I guess you got a point there."

And that was when I saw the arrow on the little compass he had mounted on his dashboard start going crazy. Inside the clear plastic window, the directions spun round and round.

"What the hell?" he said. "You see that?"

"I see that."

"What's wrong with it?"

"How would I know?"

But I did know. My gaze had inadvertently settled on the black ball of a compass and without knowing it, I'd set it spinning. The sorahein, of course. Its effects had obviously not worn off yet. Not completely, anyway.

"Could you hit the heater?"

"Huh?"

"I'm cold."

"Oh." Then he glanced over his shoulder at me and gave me a big seriocomic frown. I probably wasn't being a very good guest, being so demanding and all.

"They got guards all over the place."

"I know."

"And hidden cameras."

"I know that, too."

"They'll find you."

"They'll try, anyway."

"And then they'll find out who helped sneak you in."

"If they do find me, I'll tell them the truth."

"That I had nothin' to do with it?"

"No. That you masterminded the whole thing."

He didn't find me very amusing.

"You jerk," he said.

"I need some more heat back here."

"You've got guts, I'll give you that."

"Which flowers are for the White House?"

"There're little cards on each spray. Saying White House. Smart guy like you should be able to figure that out."

1600 Pennsylvania Avenue came into view. It's impressive, and I say that as somebody who's seen it a few thousand times. It's impressive and it means something and even a cynic like me can get the occasional goosebump when he contemplates all that the White House stands for. Not even the entire United States Congress has been able to besmirch what it stands for, though, God knows, it has tried hard enough.

"Pull over there. To the curb."

"Why?"

"Why do you think? We're going to trade clothes."

He glanced over his shoulder. "You going to shoot me?"

"Not if I don't have to."

There was plenty of rope in the back of the truck to tie him up with. I made a gag from the rags and then hit him hard enough with the Walther to keep him out for a long time.

After I had struggled into his uniform, I covered him up with my clothes to keep him warm, and then I climbed up to the driver's seat.

I swung the truck left and pulled up to the gate.

Brakes squeaked.

I rolled down the window. The guard with the clipboard looked at me and said, "Where's Don?"

"Bad head cold."

"Who are you?"

"I work in the greenhouse usually. I was the only one who had any free time, so Mr. Runyon put me on delivery."

"Bad time for a head cold, Christmas and all."

I was scanning him but not getting anything especially helpful. He was having a brief debate with himself. Was I for real or not?

I couldn't afford to let him choose wrong, and I didn't have time to let him decide before acting, so I did something I'd never done before.

Counting on the sorahein to help me, I reached out and sort of influenced his thoughts.

"You say hello to Don for me," he said.

"I sure will."

The gates parted. He waved me on inside.

Elated and shaken, I drove straight to the proper area. I was shaking badly. Suddenly, and for the first time in years, I was afraid of my own powers.

33

After figuring out which of the flowers to carry inside, I passed by yet another guard and then reached the interior of the White House.

I spent a few minutes reorienting myself, remembering everything I'd seen here yesterday.

Several men in blue suits wound their way, in a tight pack, out of one room at the end of the hall, then wound their way right back into another.

I started walking around. I covered a good portion of my face with the huge centerpiece of evergreens and holly and ribbons I was carrying. Buried deep inside was the Smith and Wesson with its two special bullets. That was all Finebaum had time to make. I also had my Walther in there, just in case.

Special assistants fluttered past me; somber portraits of past Presidents gazed down upon me with lofty disdain; a few people muttered good mornings and I muttered right back at them.

I glimpsed the Vice President, a garrulous man who always reminds me of the leading man in a dinner theater play; he was giving instructions to a secretary and then yawning and then walking off.

Most doors were decorated with holly wreaths this morning, and the air was tangy and sweet with the scent of several small and fully decorated Christmas trees. There was a faint air of jubilation, the kind I remembered from my grade school days—Christmas was almost here. Which meant several long, lingering days off.

Today there was no time to be impressed with the shine and sheen and history of it all.

I was here on a pretty singular mission.

I reached the Oval Office.

The door was ajar.

I looked left and right, the way my mother had taught me to cross streets, and seeing nobody I peered in past the parted doors.

There was the baronial desk used by most of the Presidents since Dwight Eisenhower. But unfortunately, nobody was sitting behind it. The office was empty.

"Is there something I can help you with?"

He was some kind of security person. Had to be with the blue suit that looked a little less tailored than most of the blue suits you saw in these halls, and the scar running to the left of his cleft chin, a scar he'd gotten in some kind of combat, most likely during his tenure as a cop.

I smiled. "I guess you caught me."

"Caught you?"

"I'm filling in for Don. The regular guy? Anyway, I'm supposed to deliver these flowers, and I knew that the Oval Office wasn't far away so I just decided to sneak down the hall and take a peek at the Oval Office."

"This is the White House. You don't 'sneak' anywhere."

"I'm sorry. I knew I shouldn't have done it."

"Which gate did you come through?"

"The one they told me to, at the flower shop, I mean."

He whipped out a small walkie-talkie, thumbed a button and said, "Gate B, this is Hamilton. Do you know about a delivery man for—" He paused. "What's the name of the florist's?"

"Sterling," I said.

He thumbed the button. "For Sterling Florist?"

A scratchy voice in the tiny black box: "I sent him through. He's substituting for Don, the regular guy."

"All right. Thanks."

"Is there a problem?"

"No problem," the security man said and then clicked off. To me, he said, "Where do the flowers go?"

"Right on that table over there. At least that's where I think they go."

"Good. Go set them down and then I'll walk you out."

"That's nice of you, thanks."

So he walked me over to the fancy Edwardian table beneath the fancy Edwardian mirror and I set the flowers down and arranged them in the way I imagined a florist would, and then he touched my elbow and said, "Let's go."

So we went.

Back down the fine and shiny corridor where so many famous Americans had trod, back past the gallery of famous Presidents, and then toward the gray morning light filling the double doors at the bottom of three steps.

I reached out for him mentally, but this time it didn't work. I was too tired, or his suspicions had raised his subconscious shield, or maybe both. Whatever, even with the sorahein singing in my veins, I couldn't influence this guard. He was going to walk me right out of here and there wasn't anything I could do about it.

I reached the first step and he said, "Next time they're going to substitute somebody, you tell them to call not only the gate but White

House security—in advance—and tell us about it, all right?"

"I sure will. And listen, I really am sorry, you know, about sneaking a peek and all."

His beeper went off. Loudly. The two guards standing just inside the entrance door at the bottom of the steps looked up idly, making sure that what they heard was really a beeper. Then they turned away and looked back at the White House grounds.

The security man said, "Yes."

"Some kind of disturbance on the second floor. Jockson's office. One of the secretaries started screaming. Check it out."

"Yessir."

The security man, all urgency now, nodded to the stairs leading down and said, "You get the hell out of here now, you understand?"

"Yessir."

I turned obediently toward the steps just as he took off jogging in the opposite direction, his pockets jangling coins as he ran.

The guards were still looking outside, away from me.

The security man had disappeared.

This was the last opportunity I would likely get to do what I needed to do.

I did my school-crossing left and right routine and then set off walking quickly back toward the Oval Office. Then I remembered the Smith and Wesson I'd left tucked deep inside the centerpiece.

I went over to it, stuffed my hand deep down the center, grabbed the gun, shoved it inside my belt, and then started walking even faster.

Three sweaty minutes later, I reached the Oval Office. I was just starting to peek past the parted doors again when I heard a voice coming around the corner. The voice belonged to the President.

There was a closet behind me and six feet away. I got to it only moments before the President and Vice President came around the corner and reached the Oval Office.

In the darkness, for what seemed to be at least an hour, I waited for my chance to come.

But he was long-winded, our President, and not a soft-spoken man, either, so even though I was inside a closet I could hear him holding forth on many vital issues.

He spoke very well for an alien.

34

In real time, the Vice President stayed in the Oval Office approximately fifteen minutes. When he left, he said, "We're still meeting those astronauts at 4:15, right?"

"That's the plan," said the President.

"Good. I'll go tell my secretary. She wants me to sign some things anyway. I'll be right back."

He stepped crisply away. He had a kind of golf-pro elegance that made middle-aged ladies swoon.

I didn't have much time.

I had to get into the Oval Office, shoot the President, and make my escape in just a few minutes. I started thinking about what Pam had said, about there being no way I could escape, and I got scared. In the abstract, I'm all for making the noble gesture, but in the specific, I'm not sure I'm all in favor of me being the vehicle for such nobility.

But it was too late.

Nobody else was around to do it, and this might be the last chance the human species would ever have. (I spent a minute trying to think of all the good things humankind had wrought—medicine, music, painting, things like that—because I knew that if I started thinking about the Holocaust and the man-caused famines in Africa and the murder rate in the United States, I just might decide that the human race wasn't worth saving after all.)

I eased open the closet door. Peeked out. The old left and right routine again.

The corridor running past the Oval Office was empty. The Vice President had left the doors ajar. Apparently the President liked them that way.

An enormous silence had descended on this wing of the White House, almost as if everyone were subconsciously holding his breath in anticipation of what was about to happen.

A grandfather clock tolled the hour; a helicopter passed overhead and flew away eastward, distant now.

I stepped into the corridor.

I slid the pistol out from my belt.

I reached the parted doors of the Oval Office.

I peered inside.

The President stood at the window, his back to me. He was a tall man, in reasonably decent trim, and this particular angle in this particular light would have made a good photograph—the President contemplating the problems facing all humankind. Would have made a nice touch in a thirty-second TV commercial.

My senses were starting to jump with the energy and thoughts I was picking up from his mind.

Alien thoughts—

A unity, a sense of oneness, I'd never imagined possible.

A seductiveness to that absence of pain and loneliness that almost made up for the corresponding absence of love and joy.

A sense of vastness, and of power, and of imminent fruition.

He turned.

I hadn't expected that.

He turned and saw me there, my weapon ready, and said, "Oh, shit. You're going to kill me, aren't you?"

My mind bristled with the alien presence and images my scan was picking up.

I thought of Lee Harvey Oswald, and the man who shot McKinley, and the woman who tried twice to shoot President Ford.

If the human race endured, I might very well find myself grouped in with them. Maybe I'd kill the President and the aliens would withdraw and nobody would ever believe me or Pam about the President being an alien. Maybe I'd just be the guy who killed the President.

He stood there in his blue suit and white shirt and blue tie and said, "You don't know what's going on here."

"That's the problem," I said, advancing into the room, past the fireplace, past the facing sofas, past the desk. "I know exactly what's going on here. And that's why I have to kill you."

"Look, you stupid bastard, you really don't know what's going on here—"

Maybe if he hadn't been so condescending, I would have let him live a little longer.

The silencer was a lot more efficient than I thought it would be. Just two tiny rumbling noises and then silence again.

I shot him twice in the belly.

For a long moment, his gaze held mine. When he collapsed, it was all at once.

And then he was dead.

I started across the floor to him, to make sure he was dead, when I heard two voices coming down the hall behind me.

Before I had time to scan the dead President, I turned and started looking around for a place to hide.

Nothing recommended itself.

The voices reached the closed doors of the Oval Office then paused as hands gripped the doorknobs and the doors were opened and—

President Bob Haskins looked at me and said, "What the hell're you doing in here?"

And then his eyes followed mine to the President Bob Haskins who lay on the floor appearing to the untutored eye to be very very dead.

A smirk appeared on the face of the President standing in the doorway. He nodded to the Vice President, who now checked out the dead man on the floor next to me.

The Vice President started smirking, too.

President Haskins glanced at me and shook his head. "You stupid bastard, you shot my double."

At first, I thought he might be joking, but then I remembered that many state leaders used doubles, everybody from Hitler to Churchill. And in several instances, the doubles had gotten themselves assassinated.

As had apparently happened now.

All this work to kill President Haskins and now—

Our gazes locked. I saw the orange lights flare so brightly within his eyes, and then I felt a tremendous blow fall upon my mind.

I had no time to raise a defense, and no strength to block it with anyway. The alien was simply too strong.

I felt a wave of blackness rise up and wash over me, and then I collapsed right next to the President's double.

35

December 23

They had docked at the space station *Freedom* amid a grand ceremony of welcome and celebration. Colonel Jacobs, Miriam Goldmann, and Feodor Varnov had given kisses to everyone on the station. Now they were on board a shuttle, en route back to Earth.

But Wendy paid no attention to this. All she could see was the mild rash she'd developed on her inner forearms. All she could think about were the dreams she'd been having—sometimes even while she was awake.

In her dreams, she was different people. She'd been Cap'n Jack Campbell; she'd been Colonel Jacobs and Feodor Varnov. She'd even been President Haskins, looking in a mirror and laughing at the orange light reflected in his eyes. She'd been people she didn't know, people she'd never heard of, and yet through it all she'd been herself, and more than herself.

Wendy didn't know what was happening, and none of her crewmates would talk to her. Even Miriam, who had returned to the control room after a couple of days, silent and subdued, hadn't spoken a word. The five of them seemed to be able to communicate without speaking, almost as if each one knew what the others were thinking.

It was frightening, but at the same time there were moments when it seemed almost attractive.

Colonel Thompson, the shuttle commander, was busy flying his ship. Miriam, seated on the acceleration couch next to Wendy's, suddenly turned to her, a dull orange light flickering in her eyes.

"You're fighting us, Abronowitz."

"What?" Wendy felt tired, her mind slow and sluggish.

"That's never happened before. Only Cap'n Jack has been able to stay apart, and that was because of his tattoo. You don't have a tattoo, do you, Abronowitz?"

Wendy frowned and shook her head, trying to make sense of this. A tattoo? Of course she didn't have a tattoo. Her mother would never . . .

She lost the train of thought. It was too hard

to concentrate, too hard to try to make sense of things. Better to just let go.

She fell asleep, her head lolling against the bulkhead, dreaming of Colonel Jacobs, President Haskins, Cap'n Jack Campbell, and all the others.

"That's right, Abronowitz," Miriam said. "Don't fight it. It won't do you any good anyway."

36

I was in a room, a dark room that smelled of coffee and furniture polish, a dark room with a draft from a rattling window I could not see.

A voice said, "Are you awake now?"

"Pam?"

"Yes."

"Where are we?"

"On the second floor of the White House."

"I smell coffee."

"The janitor has a Mr. Coffee."

"How did you get here?"

"When you didn't come out, I went up to the gate. Apparently, the guard had been told to watch for me. He took me inside and then they put me in here with you. I don't think they've figured out how to get rid of us yet."

"Oh?"

"A lot of publicity if an astronaut's wife turns up dead alongside a psychically gifted man on the public payroll."

"I see what you mean."

"You want some coffee?"

"How can you see in the dark?"

"I can't. I'll just pull back the shade."

I smiled. "For every complex question, there's a simple solution."

"You think they'll really kill us?"

"No. I think they'll infect us. Probably just as soon as this thing with the astronauts is over with."

"The astronauts?"

I told her what I'd heard. I saw no reason to mention that I was sure she'd already been infected.

She went over and hiked the curtain back. Gray winter light pressed against the ice-rimed window. "I'll hold the curtain. You do the pouring."

We were in a square room filled with neatly arranged brooms and brushes and dustpans and vacuum cleaners and large bottles of floor wax and small bottles of window cleaner.

I stood up. My head pounded. Whatever weapon the President had put me out with had certainly been effective.

"Cream?"

"He has real cream?"

"Well," I said, "powdered creamer."

She laughed. "Not much of a last meal, is it? Two cups of coffee and not even real cream."

I stood at the window, looking down. "That's where they'll come in."

"Where?" she said, moving closer. She smelled great, her perfume and her skin and her hair, and this was a dopey time to become aware of her sexually.

"Right down there. That entrance where the guards are. An hour or so from now there'll be two or three long black limos pulling up and the six astronauts will be there."

"The reception's downstairs?"

"Right."

She touched her head to my arm. "You tired yet?"

"Too scared to be tired."

She smiled. "Me, too."

We stood there that way, her leaning against me, and my senses filling up with all the various sweet scents of her, and I said, "I'm not picking up anything. In my mind."

"Nothing?"

"Whatever they knocked me out with seems to have stunned my psi powers, too."

"Not even any static?"

"Not even static. And that's strange."

"What is?"

"When I was in the back of the van sneaking in here, I was able to stare at this compass the driver had mounted on his dash and make it go really crazy so it wasn't true at all. I've heard of that being done before, but I never saw it firsthand and I sure never thought I'd be able to do it myself."

"But you were? You're sure?"

I nodded. "Yes, and I know it was the sorahein, too. But after Haskins hit me with that blast—nothing."

She sat on the edge of a barrel, staring at me. "Put your coffee down and look at me."

"What?"

"Concentrate on me. See if you can scan me at all."

"It won't do any good. I'm not picking up anything."

"At least try."

I sat my coffee down, fixed the shade so that it offered a small angle of light, and then concentrated on Pam, who stood in the center of the dusty closet looking as if she were about to be beamed up.

"Anything?" she said after a time.

"Nothing yet."

"Try harder."

"All right, boss."

But there really was nothing. There were times before when my powers had gone—and I remembered the almost embarrassing feeling of trying to scan somebody and getting absolutely nothing at all. I felt like a charlatan stage magician or something.

"Anything?"

"Huh-uh."

"Damn," she said.

"You sure seem uptight."

She paced a little then turned to me. "There's something I haven't told you."

"About what?"

"About the sorahein."

"What about it?"

"I didn't give it all to you. I only gave you half."

"That pisses me off."

"I'm sure it does—but I didn't want you to die. I was afraid for you."

Now it was my turn to pace around the closet. "You had no right to do that."

"I know. And I apologize." She hesitated. "I was hoping your powers would come back. That's why I just had you try to scan me."

"Well, it didn't work."

"I know."

She went over and sat on the edge of the barrel again. "You can have it if you want it."

"You still have it?"

"In my purse."

"Dammit, that belongs to me, not to you."

"I know. I just don't want anything to happen to you."

"I want you to give it to me now."

"I'm scared."

"I don't give a damn what you are, Pam. I want the sorahein. All of it that's left."

And then she was in my arms and I was feeling all sorts of conflicting things, but mostly I was giving in to the simple warm pleasure of holding her this way.

She was crying. "Jack's gone. He'll never come back to me. Not now. I don't want you to desert me, too. I couldn't handle it. Not now."

Gently, I said, "I have to take that sorahein. It's the only chance we've got."

"Hold me for thirty more seconds."

I laughed. "How about twenty-five?"

I shut up and held, which was what I'd wanted to do anyway. I even closed my eyes and realized with a kind of tender pain how long it had been since I'd really cared about anybody but myself.

"This is a lot more powerful than sorahein," I said.

"I know."

I held her some more, smelling her hair, girly and clean and redolent of silk slips and sachet and moist kissable lips.

Reluctantly, I eased her away from me. "I'll lie down on the floor and you give it to me."

"This may be too much—you know, both halves in this small a time."

"We'll have to chance it."

To that, she said nothing.

She knew just as I did that this was the only hope we had.

37

A stretch limousine brought the six astronauts from the airport to the White House. Two policemen on motorcycles with flashing red lights preceded them. In the whipping snow, and the darkening afternoon, the policemen looked very cold.

Inside the limousine there was very little talk. A man from the White House press office, a man clearly not a part of things, asked innumerable questions and received, for his trouble, innumerable silences.

Finally, he looked embarrassed and started staring out the window at the D.C. skyline.

Colonel Jacobs sat next to Wendy. Jacobs was very relaxed. With its bulletproof glass, three phones, TV set, wet bar and built-in CD system, this was the car to relax in.

None of them talked. If her crewmates were communicating at all—and Wendy was sure they were—it was without words.

They hadn't talked much before leaving the space station; and they hadn't talked at all once they boarded the shuttle.

From the relaxed Colonel Jacobs to the gentle welder Varnov, they sat in the limousine staring at nothing, saying nothing, an occasional pulsing of orange light appearing deep in their eyes.

Wendy feared that she would soon be one of them.

It was as if she were about to come down with a terrible cold and her entire body knew it and was just waiting for the worst of it to start.

The lethargy of a few days earlier had vanished. Wendy suspected that, by now, she should be fully a part of whatever it was that had claimed her crewmates. She had no idea why she remained apart, and from the curious glances she got from time to time, neither did anyone else.

But Wendy didn't care so much why she was still herself. She was just worried about how long she would be able to remain little Wendy Abronowitz.

She trembled suddenly, and the chills ran down the length of her body. She felt nausea and a kind of wild panic, knowing that her essence—individuality, soul, whatever you cared to call it—was being stolen from her.

She wanted to hold out, to give Jacobs and

the others the sense that she was one of them, and yet reserve enough of herself to warn people at the White House what was going on.

Her trembling became violent shaking.

The others looked straight ahead, faint light pulsing in their eyes.

Only Miriam took notice of what was happening to her.

She patted her maternally on the arm again and said, "Won't be long now, Abronowitz. A few minutes at most." God, the worst of it was that she still sounded just like the old Miriam Goldmann.

And the wild panic filled Wendy's chest again.

They still had a long way to go before they reached the White House.

And by the time they arrived, she would no longer care about warning anybody.

Because by then she would have been transformed.

And by then she would no longer be fully human.

"Don't fight it, Abronowitz," Miriam said.

And then, like the others, she angled herself back into position and resumed staring straight ahead while tiny pieces of orange fire flared in her eyes.

38

We found several feet of tarpaulin and stretched it out on the floor. It smelled of ancient dust.

I lay down and closed my eyes, waiting for Pam to dispense the sorahein, and suddenly a terrible sense of dread came over me.

True, the sorahein would greatly enhance my psi powers, but it would also bring back the paranoia and the chills and the booming relentless noises that had almost deafened me before. For a moment, I felt raw fear.

Pam opened her purse, found the sorahein.

She took the vial and poured it into the small plastic medicine cup she'd used before. "Ready?"

"Ready."

"Here goes."

"You remember what we need to do? In case I—"

"You'll be fine."

"I hope you're right. Then we'll need to go get some syringes."

"For the—"

I nodded, not wanting her to say it out loud. "Thanks for watching over me."

"Somebody's got to."

I was going to tell her how much I liked her, but she must have seen it coming.

"How about shutting up so I can pour this down your mouth?"

I smiled. "You're quite a woman."

"And you're quite a guy. Now for the last time, shut up."

I shut up.

She brought my head up gently from the tarpaulin, then guided the medicine cup to my lips.

I was sixteen years old and my girlfriend had just told me that she'd fallen in love with someone else on her family vacation.

I was seventeen years old and watching a high school homecoming bonfire. Chill autumn night; harvest moon; the brassy good cheer of the marching band; and me filled with this idiotic rush of well-being.

I was eighteen years old and spending my first night at the dormitory where Lab students stayed. No well-being filled me now—only fear. I wanted to be special. I know that sounds vain but it's true. I wanted to be special and was sensible enough to know that the only way I'd ever be special was if my psi powers continued. And here I'd done poorly on one of the first tests they'd given me. "You need to relax," the instructor said, after testing me on the random event generator. But what if it wasn't just nerves? What if I was already losing my powers?

And then the noises

screams and laughter
and   screams
and ROARING and

"Forty-five minutes."

"What?"

"You were unconscious forty-five minutes."

"Oh," I said.

"Why don't I help you sit up?"

"I'm not sure that's a good idea right now. I mean I—"

"They're here."

"The astronauts?"

"Yes. Downstairs."

"The ceremony's started?"

"Well, I saw CBS and NBC trucks pull up

down there. There must be something going on."

I was sweating and yet I had the chills; I was superconscious of my surroundings (the smell of wood shavings on a drill bit; the brilliant glassy eyes of a wren perched on the window ledge; the sounds of the pipes in the walls) and yet I felt exhausted and dulled, too.

"We need to get those needles," I said.

"I know. God, you look so weak. I hate to ask you to help."

"Just get your arm under mine and help me get up."

"I'm really sorry."

"Quit apologizing," I said.

It took three tries to get me upright and then I wasn't upright at all, or not strictly erect anyway. I sagged at the knees and I would have fallen over if Pam hadn't kept her arm around me.

And all the time I was being bombarded with sensory information and impressions—

It was a kind of insanity.

"Ready?" she said, nodding to the door.

"Ready."

At which point, I promptly slumped forward. I would have fallen on my face if she hadn't gotten her arm around my waist.

"Maybe we'd better wait a few minutes."

"Yeah," I said, grinning at her. "Maybe we had."

We waited ten minutes, actually, and then we tried again.

She walked me over to the door.

We stopped and I looked down at the lock. The door had been locked with a key from the other side.

"Don't say anything for a few minutes," I said.

She smiled. "Is that the same as 'shut up'?"

"Along the same lines."

I had my silence, or at least as much silence as I could grab while my head was filled with five or six random sounds simultaneously.

I stared at the lock.

The Lab used to show films of stunts like this. After each screening there would be a lot of debate about whether what we'd seen was legitimate. There was a lot of fakery and theatrics in our particular field.

I sure hoped that at least one of the films had been real because I was now trying to do what those psi practitioners had allegedly done.

I stared at the lock, then closed my eyes once I had properly imaged it in my mind. This is what the Lab folks had always suggested we do. Paint a picture of the object in our minds and then work with the picture.

I began to fiddle with the interior of the lock, now vivid on the view screen of my mind.

It was a pretty good lock, a tubular model with an encased dead bolt that was attached to the locking mechanism. Even King Kong would have had trouble punching his way through this particular model.

I mentally began to move the locking mechanism from left to right. I became focused enough on my task that all but the echoes of extraneous sounds and sights began to fall away.

There was just the locking mechanism. And me.

And it moved.

Not right away. And not in one easy motion. But it did move in a series of milli-inch jerks, the way something long in need of grease moves.

I opened my eyes, reached out for the doorknob, and pushed the door open.

She came into my arms for a little celebratory hug, which I was only too happy to give, and then we walked quietly into the hallway.

We knew what we needed to do.

There wasn't much time.

39

The important ceremonies were held in the East Room of the White House. Ground floor.

Fluted pilasters, Bohemian cut-glass chandeliers, four marble mantels and some of the most elaborate plaster ceiling decorations in history all reminded visitors that self-indulgence was not unknown to democracies, either.

In just the past year alone, the East Room had feted a king, two duchesses, a sultan, three heads of state, an alcoholic sports hero, a bisexual cardinal, a thirty-two-year-old virgin and at least one ambassador who had a man named Adolf Hitler as his godfather.

Today the fates were feting astronauts.

There were six of them and they filed into the vast room, a little shy about all the cameras and the sudden applause led by the Vice President of the United States.

Long tables of canapes and raw fish and sugar cakes and red wine and apple chunks and grapes were spread out in the back of the room. The Senators and House members gathered here had long been at work on the tables, especially the sugar cakes and the wine. The relatives—moms, dads, brothers, sisters, uncles, aunts, cousins, everything it seemed but pets—were too excited to eat or drink.

President Haskins, striking that strutting military pose he always assumed around members of the armed forces, walked down the row of astronauts shaking hands and offering his congratulations.

Finished with this ritual, he turned to the guests and said, "This has been one of the most technologically important manned missions ever. More useful data has been collected and brought back than ever before and these are the people responsible for it."

With this, he offered the astronauts a salute. They saluted him right back.

And then the President led all the guests in applauding the astronauts once again.

Five minutes later, as the press attained an orgiastic frenzy, President Haskins said, "Now let's enjoy ourselves with some food and drink and some very good friendship."

The reception was in full swing.

One male Senator was already figuring out which sweet little aide he was going to hit on, while one female Congressperson wondered how she was going to score some coke for her party tonight, and a reporter wondered if the congressional liaison across the room had any of the blackmail money he owed said reporter.

It was a very nice group of people, of the sort one can find only in Washington, D.C.

And Wendy Abronowitz?

Impossible to tell.

She just stood off to the side of one of the food tables, watching, watching, a kind of glazed look to her eyes.

40

We found a medical office around the corner from the storage closet where we'd been kept. The place was small, white, and orderly. One long cabinet contained various instruments doctors used. There were tools for eyes, ears, nose, throat and one that, having had a few prostate problems in my life, I didn't even want to guess at.

There were four such offices throughout the White House. Shortly after the failed attempt on President Clinton's life a few years back—I remember reading this—federal officials foresaw the day when some terrorist group stormed the White House. Thus, these small, self-contained medical clinics, ready for any emergency.

We divided up the cabinets and drawers. All I found for the first few minutes were more doctorly tools.

"Maybe they don't keep any around here,"

Pam said, opening and closing drawers frantically.

"They keep everything else," I said, desperately opening and closing the drawers on my side of the room.

Then I said, "Turn that light off." I put a warning finger to my lips.

She leaned over, turned the light off.

Office was dark. Office was silent.

The sorahein had enhanced my normal hearing range so much that I could hear the person coming from twenty yards away. I could even hear the beat of his heart. Very fast beat. He was hurrying somewhere.

He wore the blue uniform of the White House security force. He came striding by, the leather of his holster rig creaking, his well-creased trousers making small *whisking* sounds as he walked.

He glanced into the medical office, saw that it was dark, heard no noises, and passed by.

I counted to one hundred before I said, "Maybe we'd better look with the lights off."

"I agree."

We went back to work and a few minutes later, Pam found them. She looked like a six-year-old who had just gotten an A in school and was holding up her report card for inspection.

"Great," I said.

From one of the cabinets I took a flashlight

and trained the beam on the two hypodermic needles she'd placed on the desk. They were still in plastic wrappers.

"Will these do?"

"These will do great," I said.

"You want the cadmium now?"

"Please."

From her purse she took the eight-ounce bottle of cadmium that had been taped to the wall in Dr. Finebaum's motel room.

"This is kind of scary, isn't it, what we're going to do, I mean?"

I leaned over and kissed her on the cheek. "We'll both do fine."

"Just explain it to me one more time."

"Sure."

I set the bottle of cadmium down and then said, "There's a cafeteria on the first floor."

"Right."

"I sneak in there and get us white coats, like the help wears."

"Right."

"And then we pick up trays so we can kind of hide our faces behind them."

"Right."

"And then we walk into the East Room and work our way up real close to the President and this Captain Linda Baxter—who I'm sure will be there somewhere—and then you take one of them and I'll take the other."

"And we just stab them with these needles."

"Right."

"Just jab it right in?"

"Just jab it right in."

"And they'll go crazy?"

"Well, your husband certainly reacted badly to the cadmium. He went insane and then went into total withdrawal. And he had the cadmium before the parasite ever entered his body. I'm hoping that with the parasite already in them, the President and the other astronaut will react even worse."

"And then?"

I sighed. "Most likely, then we die at the hands of the Secret Service. But we just might have saved our race."

She didn't say anything for a minute. Then she said, "I guess we should go."

"I guess we should."

"I'm sorry I'm such a chicken."

"I'm just as big a chicken."

"You're really scared?"

"Sure I'm really scared. Who wouldn't be?"

We left the medical office, closing the door behind us. There was a back way to the ground floor, one that would take us very close to the cafeteria.

The din from the East Room was faint. Every once in a while you would hear sudden sharp laughter or applause.

We found the back stairs. We were halfway down them when I picked up the image: FBI men. Four of them. Two coming from behind us. Two lurking just around the corner from the bottom of the stairs. A perfect trap.

The ones behind us appeared at the top of the stairs suddenly.

"Stop right there," said the one in the blue suit with the gun while his friend wearing the brown suit and the gun nodded ominously.

The other two appeared at the bottom of the stairs.

There was no choice but to bolt. I couldn't worry about Pam, not now. One of us had to escape so the job could get done.

My first thought was to do something fancy with my psi powers, but then I remembered how difficult opening the lock had been. There wasn't time now.

I turned, scanning the minds of the two men behind me.

Can't shoot. Too many guests. Don't want to alarm them.

This was from my friend in the brown suit. He had been given these instructions by the President himself.

"Run," Pam said, "run!"

She knew that the job had to be done, too.

I put my head down and charged down the

stairs. The two men waiting there had plenty of time to get themselves in position to tackle me.

What they hadn't counted on was my stopping on the third step from the bottom and kicking one of them in the jaw and the other in the face.

I dove the rest of the way down the stairs. I had a little bit of freedom while they collected themselves and fanned out to follow me.

I turned the nearest corner, smelling the meal that the cafeteria had served for lunch. Clang and clatter of pans and dishes; janitor mopping the cafeteria floor, banging his mop handle against chair legs as he went.

I ducked inside. The janitor's back was to me. He was wearing small black headphones.

I glanced around the cafeteria. Long tables stretching in either direction. Empty chairs.

I came up from behind him, hit him hard on the side of the head. He started to collapse but got a kind of second wind so I had to hit him again. This time he crumpled. I dragged him over to a storage closet and traded him clothes. Too bad the security man had torn away my sleeve. It would have been a fairer trade with my sleeve intact.

They burst into the cafeteria moments later, the two who'd been at the bottom of the back stairs, guns drawn, faces red, eyes mean. I watched them through a louvered metal inset in the door, doing my best to influence their thoughts and send them away. A moment later, they trotted back to the kitchen, where all the noise was coming from.

Proudly wearing my new uniform, I left the storage closet carrying a whisk broom and a dustpan and looking as if I were off on an extremely important mission.

I got the hell out of there.

41

Eventually, I worked my way back to the cafeteria. I peeked through the door. Six people with their backs to me stacked dirty dishes and fed them into an outsize dishwasher. The place smelled of hot steam and soggy food.

Just inside the door and to my right was a coat hook where several white coats hung. I grabbed the cleanest one I could find, picked up a large serving tray, and hurried away.

On my way to the kitchen, I'd noticed a stack of clean glasses on one of the tables. I transferred the glasses to my serving tray and set off.

They were looking for me and they were going to find me. I was well aware of that as I moved quickly down the hall and around the corner, veering toward the East Room. Of course, they could have found me much earlier if they'd put out an alarm. But they obviously didn't want to do that because maybe I would say something to the press before the security agents could shut me up.

Just about the time I reached the East Room, the agent, a brand new one to me, filled the screen of my mind. I was sensing him maybe forty yards down the corridor. Tall, angular, crew-cutted.

He came backing out of a door, his gun drawn. He'd been searching a storage room.

I eased the tray with its jiggling glasses so that it covered a good part of my face. I hurried.

As I approached the agent, I scanned him. He saw no reason to stop me. Just another White House flunky. Not the dangerous criminal they were looking for.

Thanks to the sorahein, my hearing still amplified every sound six or seven times over. As I walked to the entrance of the East Room, the entire symphony reached me—conversation in at least six different languages, cups and glasses and silverware clanging, and laughter loud as screams.

My shoes.

Though my scan of the new agent was fading out, I did pick up his interest in my shoes— very muddy from where I'd been walking around out at the motel.

Would a proper White House employee wear shoes in this condition to work?

He was curious enough to stop me. Ask who

I was. Where exactly in the White House I worked.

He was moving fast now, and at an angle so that he could cut me off before I reached the entrance.

There was a chair by the doors. I set the tray of glasses down and turned back to the agent as if I were going to talk to him.

I kicked him hard in the groin. I dragged him away from the entrance and back to the storage room he'd been inspecting.

With his necktie, I gagged him, and with his nylon socks, I bound his wrists.

A few minutes later, I was hoisting my tray again and walking into the East Room.

An old Bob Dylan line came to mind: *All the pretty people/drinkin' thinkin' that they got it made.*

This was definitely a crowd of pretty people, movie stars, celebrated journalists, politicians, foreign leaders—and at the front of the room, President Haskins and the astronauts.

One of them, a woman with big dark eyes and short blonde hair, stood toward the back of the group and she seemed to be in pain. Instinctively, I reached out with my mind to scan her, but something blocked my probe. As one, the eyes of the five other astronauts all flared orange and they started looking around the room.

They'd noticed my scan, but they hadn't seen me yet.

I glanced around the room, too, trying to gauge just how many people there might have been infected by the number who were looking for me. I wasn't sure I could see them all, but even so there were an awful lot of them.

It was then that I began to worry about pulling off my little plan.

I moved closer. I hefted my tray and began winding in and out of small cliques of people, moving inexorably to the front.

Halfway there, I picked up somebody staring at me. The image I got was of another white-coated worker. I turned to see a stooped old man with white hair watching me. He had to be one of the oldest White House employees in history. I scanned him. He was wondering who I was. He'd never seen me before. There was no time to deal with him. I moved on.

Haskins stood at the end of a long food table. A line of people shook hands with the astronauts newly returned from the space station.

I began rearranging the food tables, squaring off all the plates so they looked orderly again, wiping up a few stains with a cloth dunked in a glass of water.

Every nerve in my body screamed for me to hurry it up, but with all of them watching for me I had to be very careful.

I reached into the pocket of my white jacket and felt the three hypodermic needles. The syringes were filled with cadmium. It would be only a matter of popping the protective caps off the needle tips and then jabbing the needle into the President's skin and then pushing down the plunger. I was going to try to save him. If it didn't work, I could only hope that Pam had escaped from the security men, too, had gotten my gun from the centerpiece, and was in the room somewhere. If I couldn't save the President, our only chance was for him to die.

I walked along the far side of the table. Neither the President nor the astronauts could see me very well because of the reception line standing between us.

An old dowager wearing a half million dollars in jewels and several dead animals around her neck was just starting to shake hands with Colonel Jacobs as I made my move.

Haskins saw me coming, sensed my intent, and tried to jerk away, nearly knocking down the dowager in the process.

She screamed and then Haskins screamed and then I leaped forward, popping the cap from the needle with my thumb, bringing the whole syringe up and then straight down toward the President's right arm.

I didn't make it. Colonel Jacobs, moving with a speed and an accuracy that startled me, pushed the dowager into my path. At the same moment, the large Russian next to Jacobs brought his hand down hard on my wrist. The syringe popped out of my grip, flying through the air and landing on the floor somewhere behind the President.

By this time, many more people were screaming and several of them were hurling themselves at me, the way a crowd always does when it isolates a madman in its midst.

I'd failed. Now it was up to Pam.

There was a sudden commotion near the French doors that led into this room. Pam was there, my Walther in her hand, but she was being held firmly by two large security guards, both of whom showed the occasional orange flash in their eyes.

My probe had alerted them, and they'd caught Pam because of it.

That was it, then. We'd lost. Whatever hope we'd had was gone, and the vaccine, if it was ever released, would come out too late.

And that's when the small blonde astronaut suddenly appeared. She rose up behind Haskins, the fallen syringe in her hand, and plunged it deep into his neck.

All of the infected people in the room let out a high-pitched, keening cry as Wendy drove the plunger home.

Instantly, everything was turmoil and chaos.

Pam took advantage of the moment to jerk her arms free, but then she looked at me, unsure what to do next. I pointed at the doors and waved her away. I knew what I had to do, and there was no way she could help me.

Most of the uninfected people in the room were reporters. They milled around, snapping the occasional photograph, asking the odd inane question, and pretty much adding to the general confusion.

I worked my way through to the President. I had to get him out. It would do no good to save him only to have him get reinfected.

The blonde caught me by the arm as I tried to grab the President.

"Do you have any more of those syringes?" she asked.

I nodded and handed her the two I had left, then turned back to the President. Out of the corner of my eye, I saw the blonde inject first a dark-haired woman whose name patch said "Goldmann" and then herself, but I had no time to ask her what she was doing. Instead, I grabbed the President and started dragging him toward one of the windows.

Behind me, the tumult was dying down. I picked the President up in a fireman's carry and went out the window. The blonde followed me out, her dark-haired friend slung over her shoulder.

Once outside, I turned back to the building. It was no longer enough to save the President. From what I'd seen, the alien had already acquired far too many people. It was too strong, and I couldn't be sure the vaccine Dr. Finebaum had mentioned would be ready in time.

Not unless I found a way to cut down the alien's numbers, anyway.

I thought of all the people in that room, all the uninfected reporters, the dowager with her jewels and her furs, the waiters with their trays. I even thought of all the infected people who could be saved with a syringe full of cadmium. But there was no choice. There was no time.

I raised my hands, feeling the sorahein pounding in my temples, and I called upon my abilities in a way I'd never called on them before.

There was a moment when nothing happened, when the keening tapered off into silence, when the guards just started to reach for their weapons, and then everything combustible in the room went up in flames. The curtains, the carpets, the seat cushions, even the clothes the people were wearing. Everything went up, and the room became an inferno.

I stayed long enough to make sure that no one escaped, and then I let the weight of my exhaustion and sorrow carry me away.

42

It turned out that even with the sorahein I had overtaxed my strength sufficiently to put me in the hospital for three days. The only annoying part of the whole business was the ringing in my ears. I was just glad that the effects of the sorahein had worn off. The ringing would have been intolerable, amplified that way.

Most of the time I watched TV. There was no official word on the aliens, which told me they were still controlling too many powerful people, but there was enough other information for me to piece together some things. For one thing, the President was safe. He'd brought in a new set of physicians, and I understood he was receiving extensive medical exams. The Vice President had been caught in the flames, and one of Haskins' first official acts after the fire was to name a successor. He chose a Senator from Ohio, who reassured us that he would do his part to keep the administration honorable and dedicated to American values and American ways, and that he hoped the press would now let bygones be bygones and quit bringing up that unfortunate affair he'd had with that fifteen-year-old cheerleader back in Boise last year.

In other words, not a whole hell of a lot had changed. We went right on, for good and ill alike, being human beings.

On Tuesday, the second day of my stay, Wendy Abronowitz came up to see me. She brought a bouquet of cheery yellow flowers, put them in a vase, and set the vase on my windowsill. They were pretty and bright and just the right touch.

"I wish they'd put *me* in the hospital," she said.

"No, you don't. The food's awful."

"Yes, but I wouldn't have all the reporters following me around asking me about what happened." She smiled. "But you'll find out what I'm talking about as soon as they let you out of here."

"The funny thing is, when I looked at you in the reception line, I figured you were one of them. All the returning astronauts had that sort of glazed look in their eyes."

She shook her head. She had a most attractive head, did Wendy Abronowitz. "I wasn't sure, either. I was starting the transformation process, but luckily I was able to hold off until we got to the East Room. I've talked with some people who think it may have had something to do with the birth control patch in my arm. And with what you've learned, we've been able to help a lot of those that we know were infected. Most of them are back to normal."

"Even Jack Campbell?"

"That's what I hear."

She gazed at me a long moment. "You all right? You look sad or something all of a sudden."

"I was just being selfish."

And I was. With Jack Campbell back to normal, I wouldn't be seeing Pam again. As I said, selfish. Not to mention petty.

Wendy leaned over and gave me a kiss with her fresh pretty face. "I'll be seeing you soon. We'll probably end up doing a hundred interviews together."

That night, a night when silver moonlight gave the snowy city a beautiful but melancholy look, Pam came up right at the end of visiting hours.

She wore a tailored gray winter coat and a smile that broke my heart.

"Hi," she said.

"Hi yourself."

"I just wanted to see how you were doing."

"Fine as can be expected for somebody like me."

She laughed. "You really should listen to one of those self-esteem tapes sometime."

She smelled of sweet perfume and cold winter night and soft melancholy woman warmth.

She took my hand. "I feel close to you in a really weird way. That's what I came up to tell you."

I squeezed her hand. "I'm going to miss the hell out of you. That's what I wanted to say to you."

"I really love my husband."

"I know you do."

"But I'm going to miss you."

I nodded and looked out at the night.

"The city seems so clean and safe on a night like this," I said. I looked at her and smiled. "I haven't even heard any gunfire for the past five minutes."

"Always the cynic."

"Not always," I said, and then I had this empty stupid feeling that I wanted to cry and I wasn't even sure why.

"I really will miss you," she said.

And then she gave me a chaste little kiss on my chaste little cheek. And then she looked like she wanted to cry, too.

"Take care of yourself," she said.

And then she was gone.

After a long time, I fell asleep and when I woke up I was still me, complete with questionable psi powers, a load of guilt, and a broken heart.

I got up and took a shower and had some breakfast and then I put on some clothes and went over to the Lab.

They were still in need of supermen, even those with a few flaws.